THE RISE OF MANIFESTO THE GREAT

A Sci Fi Comedy Where Women Wear The Trousers

KERRIE A NOOR

CONTENTS

GLOSSARY

Four Legged-Creatures :- a much talked about myth until the spaceship landed, the idea of a creature with four legs was as plausible as a woman ruling the planet.

Sex For Procreation Treaty:- unlike the quickly put together treatise of "your uterus - our survival" and "one shag one night," the sex for procreation treaty was an idea bandied about the spaceship by Wife-ie to give hope; no one thought that once landed it would come into force.

Sphere Of Energy : - a closely guarded secret handed down from Hubbie to his son. Instructions on how to light a fire without matches folded up in an empty match box; along with a few other handy formulas.

Wife-ie's Stretch and Breathe Pose: - considered by many to be the beginnings of robotic yoga, not to mention the much-whispered tantric seduction Aggie was famed for.

Bed-diving : - an act that requires neither beds nor the art of diving.

Nurturing Shed : - the tools of a nurturing shed are kept hidden from all until needed—once seen, a woman rarely opens her legs again.

The Ownership Act : - the sort of marriage most civilisations were built on.

Reflectors: - early mirrors which men blamed for the dissatisfaction of their women.

The Outlands: - a bit like the Australian outback, but with out kangaroos.

Talking Stick: - passed around like a good old fashion fag. The holding of the stick meant you had the floor and could "talk the hind leg of a four legged creature—"ad infinitum," except some took the "ad infinitum" literally, leading to the tossing of said "talking stick.".

In the end, the talking stick became as obsolete as arm wrestling, finding a home in the museum of field workers, a museum with no entrance fee as there is bugger all to see.

Turtles: - the great innovation of those in the art centre, when they grew tired of transporting things, little did they know where it would lead.

MEET THE GANG

Arthur of the North :- A small man with big ideas. The first leader and (some would say) inspiration of the whole *Manifesto the Great* saga.

Wife-ie: - A woman who is anything but a traditional wife, also the mother of Arthur of the North.

Hubby : - Wifey-ie's husband, a man who lived by his appendage, his stomach and little else.

Aggie : - a woman who took "working your way up" to a whole new level, a nobody who landed not one leader, but two.

James the Strong : - the son of Arthur of the North who, like his grandfather. believes the mark of a man is the size of his appendage and his appetite.

The librarian : - a sneaky fellow who not only runs the library, but manipulates those in power. His motto being: 'rulers a mere puppets, you just have to know which string to pull".

Manifesto the Great: - son of James the Strong (despite looking the image of his grandfather).

LM-2 : - James the Strong's second partner, she takes over where Aggie left off; some say a whole lot better.

Fanny : - the unsung hero and a creator of the "weapons of mass destruction" speech. A speech of epic boredom.

Tork: - has everything a woman could want, apart from an appendage.

Cat : - is so old, she not only remembers the landing of the space-ships, but living on one.

PART ONE

The handing down of power was something that men did, and the admiring of such powers was what was expected of women, in between looking fulfilled.

Chapter One

ARTHUR'S SEAT

"A spaceship has everything but space."–Wife-ie

Earth time: 1830s

*P*lanet Hy Man is a small planet, which, up to the arrival of Arthur of the North, was a haven for the four-legged creatures[1].

No one remembers the exact date the spaceship landed on Planet Hy Man, only that they came from some place north of the Milky Way and made Planet Hy Man what it was before women took over.

Arthur of the North, along with his sphere of energy[2], a few plans, and a set of tools, took control—although it wasn't a piece of piss, as he would later make out.

He was twenty at the time, and thanks to several treaties, a few bribes, and a keen sense of order, control was his for the taking.

Arthur of the North and his crew had been in space searching for a home for longer than they could remember.

At first, they kept a log, performed daily mind-numbing rituals, and embraced their sense of duty, which involved restraint. Space turned contraception into fertility, and after an outbreak of births, it was agreed by all on the spaceship that segregation was the only way to survive . . .

After all, the last thing you needed on a spaceship was a kindergarten.

As time progressed, the daily rituals ground the crew into a sense of pointlessness, and their sense of duty waned.

Some (mainly the women) turned to the stars, others (mainly men) chanted, and finally, most sulked.

Celibacy—the key to survival—made life as bearable as a tooth abscess. There was a limit to how much happiness a nag-free life could bring, and many missed dancing, celebrating, and singing, which without a decent fumble afterwards was as pointless as many felt their mission was.

Arthur of the North's father (a man who didn't last long on Planet Hy Man) was fed up.

The last time he'd had his conjugal rights, he had a full head of hair and a set of teeth that made mincemeat of tough bits of "pseudo-steak," and *Herself* did not answer to "Wife-ie" or "hey you" but to a selection of names he had now completely forgotten but knew put more than a smile on her face.

How long had that been? he thought.

He was casually helping himself to the ladies' leftover rations at the time, illegally picking his way through last night's roast, when he began to wonder . . . *When did all this pickling segregation start?*

He thought the log would help give some timeline to all this celibacy, and perhaps some hope.

He began to search the streamlined kitchen, which took all of two minutes . . . and without thinking, he shouted, "Wife-ie?"—a term which, thanks to segregation, was as obsolete as fresh air on a spaceship.

He looked at his Wife-ie as she entered.

She stooped through the doorway. "What are you doing here?" She sighed. "No, don't tell me, eating."

"Couldn't resist your roast. Ours is a pile of pickle—by the time I get my share, all that's left is a few bits of gristle and a dumpling you could Frisbee . . ."

He stopped as Wife-ie moved into the kitchen. His mind wandered to what was underneath Wife-ie's so-called house jacket . . .

Wife-ie stood upright with a "here we go" sigh.

She, being one of the few tall members of the crew, was always stopping and straightening in the spaceship, which would be the makings of her longevity on Planet Hy Man—and the beginnings of yoga.[3]

"Pickling mass destruction, that's what their food is." He looked at his wife. "Weapons-like . . ."

She thrust an "almost as good as home" roast potato his way with a "here" and watched as he mashed down on it.

Her hubby had the memory of an ant.

There was a time when he was as bright as the Milky Way, thought Wife-ie. Now he circles the kitchen repeating himself like heartburn.

"He's not much at the cooking, our son, is he?" she muttered.

Hubby eyed his wife; he could almost see through that jacket.

He squinted.

"Just wondering about dates and things," said Hubby. "How old am I, and more's the point . . . your ovaries?"

He tightened his squint. "Shouldn't they have retired by now?"

He gave up the squinting and went for eye contact. "We could, you know . . . engage in a little fumbling?"

A "fumbling" joke was on the tip of Wife-ie's tongue.

"I thought the log might help," he said.

"Log?"

"Yes, a quick flick might give us an idea of time and . . . your ovaries," said Hubby.

"You've the log," said Wife-ie.

"What?" Hubby choked on his potato.

"We left it with you, remember?" said Wife-ie with an unnecessarily hard slap on Hubby's back.

"Oh, that," he coughed, waving her away. "Did we not give it to you?"

She looked at his confused face.

"You're the ones hung up on records; we're to plot the stars," she said.

"Whose idea was that?" he said.

"Yours," snapped Wife-ie.

"I don't think so," he muttered.

"Ask your son," she said.

"Is he not our son?" said Hubby.

"Well, yes," muttered Wife-ie, "but he gets all that forgetfulness from you."

Hubby tried to digest the information, process it through an ageing maze-like brain, while Wife-ie, fed up repeating herself, sent a "to whom it may concern" memo.

"Someone somewhere has misplaced the log," she wrote. "And that someone is male."

The memo sent a ripple of distrust through the ship. Accusations began to fly, abusive memos were sent back and forth; all hell was about to break loose, erupt into a battle of the sexes.

Arthur of the North saw his chance.

Despite his short stature and teenage years, Arthur of the North had a persuasive power about him and soon rallied the crew into searching rather than blaming.

Finally, the log was found in an old toilet no one had used for years due to the sort of smell no amount of cleaning removed.

It was the toilet of reading matter, where the crew went when Mother Nature was not playing ball and the only cure was constipation water, which took a fair amount of sitting to take effect.

Things had improved since the constipation water days, and the toilet had been forgotten, along with its reading matter.

Late that day, segregation thrown to the imaginary wind of a space-ship, the crew sat about the table staring at the last pencil scribblings of a Gran only some remembered.

"That wasn't written yesterday," muttered one.

"Shows the pointlessness of a log," muttered another.

"As out of date as Wife-ie," muttered Hubby, which nobody chose to acknowledge.

"We could work on updating it," said Arthur of the North, "recall facts—things that happened."

"What the pickle for? We're all going to die here, who's going to read it?" muttered one.

"Yeah, who cares?" muttered another.

Wife-ie quietly flicked through the log, then slid it to her son with a "keep it to yourself" look.

With a quick scan, he slid the log into his pocket and looked at his crew.

"Maybe there is light at the end of the tunnel," he said.

"Yeah, and maybe there's a torch up my arse," said a voice from the back.

Arthur, making a mental note to *keep that so-and-so occupied,* ended the meeting.

He, under his mother's guidance, took control of all reading matter, including the log, sliding it in his underwear box where no one would dare look.

There was more to Gran's ramblings than first thought. In fact, they were anything but ramblings and could even be, as Wife-ie pointed out, the saving of the spaceship.

Gran had used the stars to plot and map the way to a planet she called Hy Man because, as she put it, men were too high and mighty to listen.

"There are planets," she wrote, "just ripe for the picking. If only that arsehole of a husband would listen to me."

Wife-ie and Arthur of the North stared at her detailed maps as clear as their so-called insipid tea.

"We've been going around in circles for years," muttered Wife-ie, "and under our noses was a map—stupid pickling segregation."

"That was Father's idea," muttered Arthur of the North.

She glared at her son.

He threw her a weak smile. "If only we worked together . . ."

She continued the glare . . .

"Like, err . . . *you* suggested."

"Exactly," muttered Wife-ie. "We'd be there by now."

Arthur of the North nodded.

"Checking may be important," she said, "but listening is everything."

Arthur of the North nodded again.

"But then again, what child listens?" muttered Wife-ie.

"I do," said Arthur of the North.

Wife-ie, ignoring her son, stared out into the dark sky.

"This must never get out," she said.

Arthur looked up at the sky, wondering what Wife-ie was staring at.

"The crew would go mental," she said.

"Have *someone*'s guts for garters." Arthur laughed nervously.

Wife-ie turned to him. "Probably yours."

---

1. *A much talked about myth until the spaceship landed, the idea of a creature with four legs was as plausible as a woman ruling the planet.*
2. *A closely guarded secret handed down from Hubbie to his son. Instructions on how to like a fire without matches folded up in an empty match box; along with a few other handy formula's.*
3. *Wife-ie's stretch and breathe poses were considered by many to be the beginnings of robotic yoga, not to mention the much-whispered tantric seduction Aggie was famed for.*

Chapter Two

THE LANDING AND HEMP

"A good landing requires more than timing."–Arthur of the North

wo days later, the spaceship landed with a bump on the dry hills of Planet Hy Man, waking all that were asleep.

Arthur of the North rolled up the blinds and was the first to see. He stared out onto a field below full of four-legged creatures and smiled to himself.

"And now it begins."

He told the others they were starting from scratch; they all laughed, apart from the voice from the back.

"Scratch?" he said. "Hardly call it scratch—you've got the tools, the maps, the templates, and that sphere thingy, which you seemed to have hogged ever since this crazy mission started."

They laughed again, almost hysterical . . . who cared? Segregation was over. There was space, glorious space.

Let the shagging begin!

They knocked up a few huts, rounded up a few hens, and then went metal producing offspring in a frenzy of maniac ecstasy.

Wind rustling through your nether regions can do that to a

cooped-up person; fresh air will send you crazy. The crew ran in the wind, built bonfires, shagged by the bonfires, the beach, the waterfalls, even up a tree—until pinecones were discovered. They were as high as Woodstock hippies, at it like rabbits, barely stopping for breath, until Arthur of the North, shagged out and panting by a hut veranda, discovered the camp was on its last egg.

The hens had escaped for what seemed the hundredth time, and there was little left from the spaceship apart from "just like steak" packets, which required opening while holding one's breath, slinging into the pan "pronto," and burning to a crisp.

The planet's atmosphere had a way of making food from the space-ship smell like a rotten egg, until all the juices were cooked out.

Arthur of the North stared out into the hills at the hens casually pecking at the grass and realized several things.

They had to build fences, perhaps kill an animal or two—which no one had ever done before—and find edible plants.

As they trolled the flat lands watching what the four-legged crea-tures ate, it was clear that the peculiar-looking grass with the peculiar smell was as natural to swallow as a mouthful of sperm.

Hemp grew everywhere and was probably the reason for the happy-looking four-legged creatures—creatures that didn't kill but spent all day chomping—and chomping, along with stomping, fertilized the hemp. As for droppings, it spread hemp like a rash in a very personal place, which was just as well, because it took quite a few whiffy week-ends before a sewage plant was installed.

One still night, Arthur of the North rose from a night of shagging, walked out into the midnight air, stared up at the Milky Way, and almost gagged.

The smell of ammonia was particularly bad that night, and as his eyes began to water, he coughed.

"We need a sewage system," he shouted.

Not even the four-legged creatures stirred; they had moved away from the smell.

Arthur of the North, clutching his box of readings, headed to the nearest mountain and sat in a cave (which was later to be christened Author's Seat until a statue was built). There was so much to plough through, and focusing on it around women was as easy as getting a word in with his mother mid rant.

He was not seen for days, reading until his eyes hurt and his skin returned to the pale-as-a-potato spaceship skin.

The crew hardly missed him; they were too busy hanging out, smoking hemp, cooking hemp, and eating the odd egg. In fact, *him* being away meant more for them and less of that mother coming around moaning about tidying up.

"Who cares if he's up a mountain?" said the voice from the back. "We can do what we like."

"Yeah," said another with a toss of an empty can.

Arthur of the North rummaged and read. It was not like he was looking to rule or anything, but if it wasn't for him, that spaceship would have been overrun with babies . . . someone had to apply a bit of order, sort things, and from what he could see, no one else was offering.

He came across many things during his readings, including Gran's rants about other spaceships. Some made him laugh, until he came across "Tracking," a chapter that had him choking on his tea.

"Shit and pickled egg," he shouted.

He'd forgotten about the *others* and their ships, and according to the readings, it wouldn't be long before his crew were tracked and followed.

He stared at his calculations; they didn't have much time.

He had to rally the crew, inspire them into caring, or else they would be overrun, ruled, bossed about, and he got enough of that from his mother.

He stamped out his fire, rolled up his template for a new statc-of-the-art recycle sewage system, cleaned up his cave, and headed back to camp.

The place was like a used football field, a bomb site. He had been away three days—it looked like three months. *Where did all the litter come from?*

The ground was littered with eggshells, hen droppings, and empty food cans and packets from the ship.

He picked up an empty "just like steak" packet curled from the sun.

Would it have killed them to pick it up?

He peered into the glazed eyes of his fellow citizens; they didn't stir. It had been one hell of a night.

"I am away five minutes and I come back to a skip," he said in his "I'm in charge" voice.

Silence.

"This place is a shambles."

"Yeah, whatever," muttered one.

"Whatever?" said Arthur of the North. "There's a bin three steps away and you're tossing trash about like ping pong balls. There'll be rats next."

A rat scurried by.

"That one's called Fredrick," muttered a comatose voice from the back.

A few chuckled.

Arthur of the North was lost for words. All he wanted was a toilet, some fresh air, perhaps a tidy place to sit. He stared at the garbage strewn across the front of the makeshift huts; it would take him days to clear the rubbish, let alone start on the john.

He began to pick things up as anger grew inside him.

Why ruin such a haven?

"We need to get ready." He tossed a few eggshells into the bin. "Other ships will come—it's only a matter of time."

No one looked up, let alone answered.

"If we don't put things in order, they'll overtake us," said Arthur of the North. He tossed a can at the bin, sending a seagull scurrying.

"So?" muttered the voice from the back.

"So? What do you mean, *so?* This camp will not be ours unless we organize, rally together."

A few blinked; some chuckled.

Arthur of the North began to fume. Could they not *see?*

"We need to sort things." He looked about, exasperated. "Look like we mean business."

A few laughed, bursting into hysterics as he, frustrated, kicked a can—unaware that it was full of pee.

"We're not on the ship now," said the voice from the back. "We're free to do what we want."

A rat raced past Arthur of the North.

He jolted, skidded, steadied himself on the bin, and toppled.

"Great pickling sperm," he roared, then stopped as he caught sight of his mother zigzagging about the urine oozing across the ground.

A few sat up, some watching, others jeering.

"Heeeere's mummy," laughed the voice from the back.

Arthur of the North righted himself.

Wife-ie pulled her son aside.

"Why are you shouting like a caveman?" she said.

"Those pickling plonkers," he huffed. "If it wasn't for me, that spaceship would have been a dustbin, completely uninhabitable, and now they're doing the same here, and I can't stop 'em."

He looked at her. "There's ships coming, you know."

"Oh, that." She chuckled.

"They'll take over," he said.

"There's no need to panic," she said.

"Panic? One look at this holiday camp . . ." He stopped. The crew were rolling joints again. *How high could they get?*

He looked at his mother. "We're sitting ducks."

She tutted. "You have to manage, not shout."

She patted him on the head. He brushed her hand away.

"How will they hear if I don't shout?"

She threw him a patronizing smile.

"I mean look at them," said Arthur of the North. "I may as well be one of those four-legged pickling creatures out in the pickling field for all the influence I have."

Wife-ie told him not to swear.

"Those rats have more say than I do."

Wife-ie told him not to exaggerate.

"You have to make *them* believe in *you*," she said.

He looked at her.

"The only thing they believe in is the size of a joint and who they're going to shag next."

"Give 'em what they want," she said.

He looked at her. "A blow job?"

She smacked him across the ear. "A promise of something better, idiot."

Arthur of the North rubbed his ear with anger.

"Better than what?" he snapped. "Shagging?"

"If you offer them something better," said his mother, "they will do what you say to get it."

Arthur of the North stared at a seagull flying by and for a moment wished it was him.

"You have to grab control before it's taken," said Wife-ie.

"Everyone knows that, Mother."

"Establish fear and then promise protection," she said.

Arthur looked as his mother's tanned features, her square jaw and lean greyhound body. She was as cryptic as a crossword, and he for one was fed up with it.

He met her steely glare with his.

"Oh, for pickle's sake," snapped Wife-ie. "Tell them the ships will come and take all their hemp. Then promise you'll protect the hemp . . ."

He stopped with an "I see, sort of" look.

Wife-ie grabbed her son's face in her hands, a gesture he always hated.

"Not only protect," she said, "but promise to control the Incomers . . ."

Arthur of the North nodded, wishing she'd let go of his face.

"Tell those bozos over there, an ordered town will intimidate the new arrivals, make 'em ripe for ordering—doing the dirty work." She laughed. "No more picking up rubbish for us lot."

Arthur of the North's face lit up with recognition.

He nodded with an "I get you."

Wife-ie smiled.

Once her son "got something," he, like his father, was unstoppable, and annoyingly single-minded.

Arthur of the North walked back to the crew, mustering all his persuasive powers and burying his anger deep into his stomach he performed a speech that had the men inspired and the women a little edgy.

Chapter Three

TREATIES

"There is no such thing as democracy, only good leaders and good systems."–Arthur of the North

*A*rthur of the North held daily meetings by the waterfall.

He sorted his male crew into the jacks-of-all-trades, the obedient or easily led, and those best kept occupied and the women into the "procreation" project.

He, well versed in Gran's readings, talked of statics, future projections, and "who does what best," which he followed up with his infamous "what women are really good at" speech, winning over the men and pissing off the women.

"Projections my arse," shouted Fanny, a girl who always stood at the front, her mother clipped her over the ear.

"We're more than a uterus," shouted another. "We are good at lots of things."

"Yeah," shouted a chorus of women.

The men jeered them.

"Just as good as you," shouted her from the back.

"Can *you* turn shit into drinking water?" shouted a jack-of-all-trades.

"Merely a sewage system," muttered Fanny's mother.

"Merely?" said the jack-of-all-trades. "What have you invented?"

"We helped with the roads," said her from the back.

"Anyone can dig," said one of the men.

The woman at the front turned on him. "Haven't seen you with a shovel."

"Why don't you shove your shovel up your butt," he hissed.

"Your butt is bigger," shouted the woman from the back.

"Up yours," shouted the best-to-keep-occupied man.

"Up yours," shouted the woman from the back.

"Up yours!" screeched a voice, sex unknown.

"We are at the beginnings of a civilization," shouted Arthur of the North over the crowd.

He fixed his gaze from one to another. "All of us . . ."

The crowd hushed. A few shuffled uncomfortably.

"And these are but temporary measures. Once our quota of babies has been reached"—he looked down at the women in a fatherly manner—"you can go back to sex when you want it." He smiled. "If you want it, that is."

The women looked unconvinced.

"You'll have all the choices men have. We just need a few babies first."

The women muttered and moaned, then agreed to go away to think.

Wife-ie suggested a treaty.

"They always work," she said. "Folk love them and no one reads the small print."

Arthur of the North wrote several treaties: the "Sex for Procreation"[1] treaty, which went down like a stink bomb, the "Your Uterus Our Survival" treaty, which infuriated the women and had the men endlessly cracking jokes, and the "One Shag One Night" treaty, which was laughed at by all.

Then he told the women they would go down in history as "those who gave their all to save the species."

The men, silenced by Wife-ie after a few "flat on your back" jokes, threw in a round of applause and cheering on a par with a football stadium as suddenly it occurred to them what the treaty meant.

"So fatherhood is out the window?" muttered one woman, the unofficial spokeswoman.

"Well, not necessarily, just put on hold," said Arthur of the North.

"Shall we say optional," muttered Wife-ie.

"Optional? And how does that work if you have no idea who the father is?" said the spokeswoman.

"Work in progress," interrupted Wife-ie.

"We'll build you some stables," said a jack-of-all-trades.

"We're not horses," said a woman who actually looked like a horse.

"Luxurious-like, with beds and things," said a jack-of-all-trades. "Perhaps a few whips . . . ?"

"Or prostitutes," said the horselike woman.

"Well, you are, essentially," muttered another jack-of-all-trades near Wife-ie.

Wife-ie slapped his head.

"Well, they are," said the jack-of-all-trades, rubbing his head.

"It's only temporary," said Wife-ie with a steely look at the man.

"You will be Earth mothers . . . for the planet," said one of the obedient, getting into the spirit of things. "With the finest hens, pick of the eggs."

The women looked at each other.

"And we'll build your stables with the best views . . . ."

"We're not horses," said the horselike woman.

"The nurturing stables," muttered Arthur of the North.

"We're not pickling horses," shouted the woman from the back.

"How about the nurturing *shed*," said a jack-of-all-trades. "And we can put it by the waterfall, here."

The woman looked about at the lush grass, the clear pool below the waterfall. There wasn't a rat in sight.

"And there'll be no sex unless you say so," said Arthur of the North.

"What?" muttered a few of the men.

"And, of course, only if the day's work has been completed," said Arthur of the North.

"You mean you're using us," muttered one of the women, "as a sort of payment for work?"

"Oh, no," said Arthur of the North. "You are in complete control." He smiled. "You have the last say."

"And it's only temporary," said Wife-ie.

The women looked at each other, unconvinced.

"Oh, and did I say you will be on hemp duty? Complete . . . control," said Arthur of the North.

"What?" shouted the men and Wife-ie.

"Yes, the women are in the best place to take care of the hemp," said Arthur of the North.

The women looked from one to the other.

"It would be nice to save the planet," muttered one.

"And have a break from all-day sex," said another.

Within days, Arthur of the North's leadership was established, not only for him, but for his soon-to-be-born offspring.

With the help of his sphere of energy, sewage plant designs, and a payment system in hemp, Arthur of the North instructed the males to build, while the women—now firmly under procreation duty—were to nurture.

Hubby and Wife-ie watched as their dwarf of a son took control like a cowboy with a wild horse, Hubby mildly confused and Wife-ie with an "I taught him everything he knows" look.

"It all started with a sewage plant," muttered Wife-ie. She turned to her Hubby. "You must be proud."

They were lying on the grass at the time staring at the clouds above.

"All those years of control and fake air," muttered Hubby.

She slid her hand into his.

"I never thought I'd see a cloud again."

She kissed his cheek.

Hubby rolled onto his Wife-ie and made himself comfortable.

"Or the sun on my back." He chuckled.

It was his last chuckle, his last words.

With several ecstatic grunts, accompanied with the sort of pelvic thrusting that would earn a porn star an Oscar, Hubby gasped his last breath and Wife-ie her last orgasm.

As he lay on top of her with a death mask of ecstasy, she patted his back.

"You've done yourself proud, my hubby," she muttered and lay there until the sun went down.

---

1. *Unlike the quickly put together treatise of "your uterus - our survival" and "one shag one night," the "sex for procreation treaty" was an idea bandied about the spaceship by Wife-ie to give hope; no one thought that once landed it would come into force.*

Chapter Four

INCOMERS

"A sewage plant is the beginning of civilization."–Arthur of the North

*T*he first spaceship arrived in the middle of Hubby's burial.

The crew—or *Settlers*, as they called themselves—had worked their socks off building, creating, even laying off sex for a while to create a town, and Arthur of the North knew a day of celebration was needed: a day for Hubby, the forefather of Planet Hy Man.

Not that many agreed with the whole forefather bit; Hubby was mainly remembered for sneaking into the women's kitchen. Wife-ie was known as the true forefather, but who was going to argue when the first batch of home brew was ready, and Hubby was a far more likeable character than crabby-faced Wife-ie?

The spaceship landed on a pad, using coordinates sent by Wife-ie— a ploy to let them know who's boss. And as the new ship opened its doors and stared onto a funeral befitting royalty, the ploy worked.

The Incomers had heard of a sewage system of superior quality, but they had no idea that there would be so much more: flowers, banquet tables, costumes, and buildings that required stairs, porches, gardens, and hens obediently caged, silenced by the drumming echoing through the main street (albeit the only street).

The Incomers realized they were too late—control was taken, a leader established—and the only thing they could do was grovel for decent positions.

The lucky Incomers were assigned to the building of the library. The unlucky Incomers ploughed roads and constructed engines, while the female Incomers were sent to the nurturing stables to live with the other women, along with the hens, which, once the drumming stopped, were as noisy as the engine room of a spaceship.

It was the women who first named them Incomers. They sent the women Incomers to do their dirty work, cleaning the hens while they "nurtured" the garden—cultivating the hemp.

Wife-ie, who considered herself above most women, took up residence in the library building hut. Calling herself head supervisor ("head annoyer," as the men called it), she facilitated the erecting of the library and, more importantly, the censoring of reading material and ever-growing treaties.

In fact, there was so much to censoring that she needed a helper or two.

Causing more than a stir, she chose two Incomer women, which, as she explained to Arthur of the North, "stopped those Settler women from getting too big for their boots."

By the time the third and last spaceship had arrived, the Incomers had certain jobs and areas to live "with a bit of a view," and the second ship's crew, known as the Foreigners, had been allocated the original huts to live in, which had moved to a site with no view.

The huts, which despite being of an inferior "thrown together" quality, were classed as a "conservation area." Which basically meant all adjustments, "add-ons," or inner reconstruction were forbidden.

The Foreigners were led there the day they arrived.

They looked about the damp space with a "so much for a warm welcome" look and said little.

"It's an honor to reside in such a historical landscape," muttered one Incomer, shamefaced.

"An honor?" muttered a small voice from the back.

"Why, yes," said the other Incomers. "This is the first settlement, where it all started."

"What, here?" muttered another.

"Well, not exactly here, but near here," said the shamefaced Incomer.

"We've come a long way since then," said the other Incomer.

"So it would seem," muttered the captain of the Foreigners' ship, dumping his overnight bag on the ground.

"Enjoy," muttered the shamefaced Incomer as the other Incomer handed the captain a "report for duty" memo.

With another "so much for a warm welcome" look, the Foreigners peered at the memo, a few swearing under their breath, apart from a loudmouth.

"Enjoy?" he shouted to the backs of the Incomers. "Are you having a laugh?"

The Incomers disappeared into the sunset without a backward glance.

"Landscape?" shouted the loudmouth. "This is as much a landscape as my penis is a vagina."

A few pulled faces.

"It's probably best to keep quiet," muttered the captain. "Keep the genitals to a minimum."

"There's bugger-all grass, the sun's blocked by that giant penis of a sewage system over there—"

"Let's just get a feel for things before we insult the locals," muttered the captain.

"—and as for the huts, one fart and they'd collapse. We'd be better off living in a pickling wheelbarrow."

"Farting will be the least of your worries if you don't shut up," said a voice from the back.

For weeks, Loud Mouth moaned, until one day, as the Foreigners lined up for work, a mission was issued—a mission so lousy, so diabolical, that no one volunteered. Instead, when someone was asked to step forward, they all stepped back as the captain pushed Loud Mouth forward.

The Foreigners worked in the production lines—the crappiest of the jobs on the planet—where they took orders from the Incomers. Their job was to make uniform building blocks, pipes, screws, and tools for the Incomers' roadworks and engines. It was so boring that many did it with their eyes closed, until a batch of blocks were made upside down, causing a major tilting of the library.

Loud Mouth was sent to "retrieve and replace"—an impossible mission that involved dealing with Wife-ie and a fair amount of shouting.

Loud Mouth, however, saw an opportunity.

"What you need is statues," he said Wife-ie. "To hold things steady."

She looked at the swarthy man, dark from production line work.

"The deadline for the opening of the library is getting near," she muttered. "Would a statue speed things up?"

"Definitely," Loud Mouth said, producing a mock-up statue of Hubby from beneath his shirt. "Art," he said, "is the very cornerstone of civilization."

Wife-ie stared at his artistic interpretation of the man she had loved and dominated.

"Oh," she said, running her fingers over mushed hemp.

"If you like it," said Loud Mouth, "I can construct a life-size one and place it here, to resolve the tilt. Your opening would be on time, and you could have *this* by the entrance—for all perpetuity."

Wife-ie was speechless. Loud Mouth wasn't loud at all; he spoke in a whisper, and with such big words.

"After a sewage plant comes many things," he whispered near her ear, "but finally art."

Wife-ie, suppressing all feelings of admiration, nodded.

"It needs to be more than life-size," she muttered. "It needs to dominate the skyline."

Loud Mouth's statue did more than that. It was huge, majestic, magical, alluding to huge things beneath his cloak and a nose large enough to picnic on.

Many stopped and stared; it was the first of its kind, its large silhouette catching the sun from dawn to dust.

"It's like his nose follows you," muttered many.

Loud Mouth was commissioned to create a second statue.

"I want one of my son," said Wife-ie, "dominating the main street, overseeing all."

Arthur of the Norths' statue was erected at the high point of the main street and so impressive that birds flew by without a dropping, rats took the long way around, and women laid flowers at the statue's feet.

Arthur of the North, moved to almost tears, made Loud Mouth the first ever statue coordinator.

"I'm just one of many," said Loud Mouth. "All us Foreigners have the creative gene."

Arthur of the North smiled to himself; that "gene" theory was as believable as fertility without men.

"We could help you create the city of your dreams," said Loud Mouth, who had moved on to a speech on art being the "cornerstone of civilization."

Arthur of the North smiled again. Loud Mouth reminded him of him, and despite protests from his advisers, he bequeathed the Foreigners an arts corner near a hillside with such a view that even Wife-ie was miffed.

"The galaxies love a trier," he said.

"Aye, but not the Settlers or the Incomers—they'll go mental," said an adviser.

Arthur, dismissing him with a wave, talked of how "Loud Mouth made his mother happy," which silenced all. Once Arthur of the North talked of his mother, there was no moving him.

The Settlers and Incomers did "go mental," sparking the "Great Hemp Riot." Hemp was stolen, huts were burnt, and accusations flew, until Arthur of the North stepped in with a "freedom for the male artist" treaty, which was as much good as a hemp roof.

The treaty was shoved onto a burning hut, and punches were threatened and about to be thrown when the third and last ship, with a loud crunching of gears, docked on the pad with a crew full of hope.

The spaceship crew's hopes were soon dashed as they were greeted with a raging mob of Settlers and Incomers now looking for anything to punch.

"Aliens," they shouted. "Let's get 'em!"

The Foreigners, with memories of their own arrival still fresh, almost pitied the Aliens and then decided to seize the opportunity.

As the Settlers and the Incomers chased both the men and women Aliens to the outlands, the Foreigners moved the three redundant spaceships to their arts corner and recycled, reinvented, and up-cycled to their hearts' content, creating furniture so amazingly comfortable that no one would ever argue about the arts corner for quite some time.

Chapter Five

ALIENS

"Celibacy is preferable to procreation sex."—Woman unknown

*I*t took ten years to create a city.

The male Settlers controlled the education; the Incomers the jobs; the Foreigners recycling, statues, and "production lines"; while women developed prolapses and soon forgot how to use a screwdriver.

The Aliens were sent to the outer lands to experiment with cropping, which they took to like they were born to it. In fact, they felt so comfortable in the outer lands that they were hardly seen—just the odd sighting at the trading post, where plants and meat were exchanged for tools or the odd bit of comfy furniture.

Soon they had developed superb farming techniques, the sort of techniques that could turn a dust bowl fertile, not that any from the city appreciated it.

In fact, Aliens were rarely acknowledged at all, let alone spoken of; their shabby treatment was quietly erased from history, until talk of a discontent in the city was heard.

The Incomers felt they were as good as the Settlers—"why can't we educate as well as be educated?" said many—while the Foreigners demanded education.

Fights began to break out, Foreigners were seen tripping up Incomers, and Incomers were seen hurling abuse at the Settlers, until Wife-ie stepped in.

With her divide-and-conquer theory, Wife-ie created Alien myths, instantly uniting the city folk in fear. "Aliens drink blood for fun" and "Aliens have the hearing of a bat" were her favorites, which she posted on lampposts and whispered into ears while dropping the price of recreational hemp tea.

Arthur of the North was impressed; hemp tea soothed even the most cynical until the "Great Hemp Riot" of eighteen forty-one.

Hemp nurturing was women's work, and it made things bearable for women, including childbirth and the many things that led to childbirth. But as recreational hemp use increased, their "prehistoric methods" were not enough.

Arthur of the North could see trouble brewing—the city was running out of hemp—and was at a loss of what to do.

Until that is, the Aliens got wind of the "blood drinking" rumors.

The Aliens' ability to spy was as spectacular as their ability to riot and being called "blood drinking morons" gave them plenty to riot about. They unleashed their much-loved horned four-legged creatures to rampage the streets like a Spanish bull run.

Arthur of the North watched the four-legged creatures knock over stalls and smash into windows. He watched as men valiantly trying to control the herd were thrust into the sky like failed matadors and knew there was only one thing he could do; bribe in the form of a treaty.

Quickly drawing up his famous "Hemp Nurturing Along With All the Hemp You Can Drink" agreement, he braved the four-legged creatures, waving the treaty like the white flag of surrender, and handed the "Hemp duties" over to the Aliens.

It was a turning point for women.

Without the inhalation of hemp ether while nurturing, women soon began to sober up, realizing how rubbish their lives were.

They spent all day mothering and producing babies with no break, no change, dealing with toddler tantrums, childhood questions about the point of existence, and teenage dramas, while men swanned in and out spreading their seed to whomever, whenever.

Soon, the women were stomping to the weekly meeting held by the waterfall waving "a penis is only the beginning" placards.

They campaigned for weeks.

The men, mildly amused, said little.

The women threatened to strike.

The men laughed.

The women locked the nurturing shed door.

The men walked away.

The women stuck "no more baby making" notes on the door, and the men, with hardly a look, jeered.

The men controlled the food *and* tools—they could starve the women into submission, and if that didn't work, they could simply cut off their hot water. *How long could a woman go without a bath?*

It was the horselike woman who came up with the manipulation idea.

"We can coerce," she said. "Talk of role models. Tell them how the Aliens do it—mold their children."

The men laughed.

"Aliens?" said one. "They dance around a fire for fun."

"Yeah, with talking sticks," said another.

"They did rampage our city," muttered the horselike woman.

Arthur of the North stopped, listened. *These women have a point.*

"Their sons go with the men all the time out there." The horselike woman gestured to the outer lands.

Sons? thought Arthur of the North. He looked at his men.

"They even bond," said the spokeswoman.

The men stopped. "Bond?"

"Yes," yelled the horselike woman. "Their motto is, 'Give me a boy at seven and I will show you a man.'"

Silence . . .

"I can see where you're coming from," said Arthur of the North. He looked at his men. "Kind of like the idea."

The men looked at each other.

"Hmm . . . molding?" said one.

"I can see how that would work . . ." said another.

It was all downhill after that, as the men took over the meeting talking of molding and shaping baby boys, building a force that could protect the city.

The women didn't get a word in . . .

Fed up and disgruntled, the women stomped home.

"All we wanted was a bit of babysitting," the spokeswoman hissed.

The horselike woman shifted uncomfortably.

"Now those bozos are going to mold our boys into *them*," said the spokeswoman.

"While we still get up every night to feed," snapped a voice from the back.

"And our girls will have as much chance as we frigging have," said the spokeswoman.

"Exactly," snapped the voice from the back.

Arthur of the North, pleased with himself, stretched out by his fire, sipping a hemp tea with Wife-ie.

"That's that sorted," he said with a smirk.

Wife-ie looked at him.

"Isn't the latest baby in there the image of you?"

Arthur of the North choked on his hemp.

"Me?"

She looked at him. "The image."

He checked his dates.

Bollocks, thought Arthur of the North, guess I have to go and bond now.

Chapter Six

WIFE-IE

"Dying well often goes unnoticed."—Scribbled in the john of a spaceship

Earth time: 1870's

*W*hen Wife-ie died, Arthur of the North was sixty and inconsolable. His mother, painful as she was, always had the best ideas, the best solutions, and it was she who kept his son, James the Strong, in toe.

James the Strong—aptly named, as he was the only man on Planet Hy Man to finish the yearly challenge of pulling a spaceship down the main street on Arrival Day—was a hard son to manage.

Very little went on in his brain apart from shagging and spaceship-pulling, which was his idea in the first place.

"What's the point of a spaceship you can't pull?" he said, and after watching him pull robustly, no one argued.

Arrival Day started a year after the Settlers arrived, causing the first of many riots that no amount of treaties could stop. The last thing the Incomers wanted to do was celebrate the arrival of the "up themselves" Settlers, while the Foreigners weren't even invited.

In the end, each group had their own Arrival Day celebrations with the promise of unlimited hemp, a day off work, and free run of the nurturing shed, apart from the Aliens.

No one had any idea what the Aliens did for celebrations. It was rumored that they treated every day as a celebration around the fire with roast veggies and a four-legged-creature race on Sunday, some say with super-strong home brew.

James the Strong, now a grown man of "forty score and whatever," had spent most of his time strutting about the place with his "head in the clouds."

His idea of thinking was staring, and his idea of a day's work was to "hang about the nurturing shed."

He had a string of women lined up waiting for his procreation seed and a string of men wondering what would happen to the city when he took over from his father.

Wife-ie dying didn't help.

She was taking ages, and it had Arthur of the North "not himself" and James the Strong no longer under her control.

Wife-ie took her time to pass on.

She was grieving the loss of Loud Mouth, her second-hand man, and would not let go until his statue was finished and erected over his cremated body.

Every morning, Wife-ie stared up from her bed, searching the eyes of Aggie, the only person she sort of trusted.

The two helpers had passed on, never really getting over the isolation caused by helping Wife-ie. Quietly cremated, their remains sat in urns in the arts corner waiting to be placed under Wife-ie's obelisk (women weren't entitled to statues).

Wife-ie's obelisk had been built six months ago when Wife-ie first took to her bed. It was built in a rush and then sat blocking a decent part of the sun waiting for Wife-ie to "kick the bucket."

The jealousy for the two helpers had passed on to Aggie, who spent her spare time avoiding "up yours" finger gestures from the other women. Being exempt from procreation duties did have its downside.

Aggie started from the bottom, a wee girl no one noticed. It was Wife-ie who saw her sitting in the corner, ignored by the other children in the shed. She lifted her up and took her home to her two helpers.

"Every woman needs one maternal experience," she said.

In truth, the two helpers were getting on a bit, and Wife-ie was always one step ahead when it came to future planning.

She looked at Aggie as memories flooded back of that pickup day. Aggie was just a thread of girl, legs like a flagpole.

She's fattened out nicely, Wife-ie thought to herself. Maybe her son would notice . . .

❖

"The future of the planet depends of you, Agnus," said Wife-ie.

"It's Aggie."

"I depends on you, Agnus," said Wife-ie.

"It's Aggie."

Wife-ie peered at her helper with watery eyes. "The statue—is it finished?"

Aggie, dabbing her master's mouth with ice, nodded.

"My Loud Mouth finally put to rest?"

Aggie nodded again.

"Just as well," groaned Wife-ie, "the last thing I need is to get up and do some shouting."

Aggie looked at her master with pity. She had as much power now as an empty packet of seeds.

"Have you checked the itinerary for his funeral?" spluttered Wife-ie with a cough.

"Yes," Aggie lied.

"I don't believe you," said Wife-ie, sparking a coughing fit; phlegm flew from her mouth. Aggie shoved a paper cup under her master's mouth like she had done a million times before.

"I want pictures." Wife-ie wiped her mouth.

"Yes, well, picture-taking requires equipment, which as we speak is in the hands of those recycling idiots, who have some stupid idea of making it sleeker." Aggie sighed. "Like that's gonna make a difference."

Wife-ie began to fidget.

"Shall I get your son?" said Aggie.

"No, he has been here every day."

Aggie nodded.

"He'll just bring that pickling awful Strong fellow. Shifting spaceships has ruined him. I told his father all that applause and shagging would go to his head, but would he listen?"

Aggie slid another ice cube between Wife-ie's lips. "Here you go . . ."

"I mean celebrating the Settlers' arrival was his stupid idea. Told him it would be a curse." She coughed, spat into her cup, and missed.

"Better?" said Aggie, reaching for a cloth.

"Now there's a festival for each pickling arrival, which always leads to a riot. I mean celebrating the day of running folk out of town—who would want to celebrate? Bound to rub some up the wrong way."

Aggie wiped Wife-ie's mouth. "Love a good riot."

"Oh, you would, wouldn't you, Agnus?" said Wife-ie.

"It's Aggie."

Wife-ie shifted uncomfortably. Why did dying have to be so scratchy?

She scratched all over despite her silky sheets. She scratched her bum, ignoring Aggie's gentle "leave it" slaps, and closed her eyes. She had no regrets.

She ran her tongue around her lips.

Aggie rubbed more ice.

"Better?" she said softly.

Wife-ie blinked at her assistant. "That library was meant for women too."

"I know." Aggie's face softened.

"You should be able to visit."

"Don't worry about that now," Aggie hushed.

"Remember the drawer." Wife-ie gestured beside her. "Take before anyone"—she coughed—"gets here."

"It's OK," muttered Aggie. "I know what to do."

Wife-ie looked at the sun streaming through the window; what she wouldn't give to see Hubby's outstretched hand pulling her to the horizon. She'd had enough . . .

She tapped Aggie's cheek.

Over the last few weeks, Aggie had nursed her, made her comfortable, listened to her . . . she was a good sort.

"I killed my Hubby," she said.

Aggie wiped her brow. "No, you didn't. You made his last moments happy."

"And now I am to follow." Wife-ie turned to Aggie. "Do you think *it* still goes on over the horizon?"

Aggie touched her cheek. She knew she was talking about sex. She always did just before she fell asleep.

Aggie offered her a pain tablet.

Wife-ie slid her hand into Aggie's and squeezed it.

A tear filled Aggie's eye.

"Don't forget the drawer," whispered Wife-ie.

A tear rolled down Aggie's cheek followed by another.

"I'm ready to go," Wife-ie murmured.

"What about Arthur of the North?" muttered Aggie.

Wife-ie didn't answer.

Aggie stared down at Wife-ie's face; was she asleep?

She waited . . . not a sound. She put her fingers under Wife-ie's nose . . . nothing. Her ear to Wife-ie's chest . . . silence.

Aggie sucked in her breath, wiped her tears, and, after one final feel for a pulse, stood.

She knew what she had to do.

She emptied the drawer, hid the contents in her room, and ran to Arthur of the North in the library.

Chapter Seven

THE LIBRARY AND THE LIBRARIAN

"If losing the hemp put all the women in the same boat, then Arthur of the North's treaties gave them the oars to row it."– Fanny

*A*rthur of the North was in the middle of a meeting, attempting to wind things up and getting nowhere fast. Concerns had been raised about James the Strong's flagrant abuse of membership, and Arthur of the North, as usual, was arguing on behalf of his son.

James the Strong was his Achilles heel. Arthur of the North chose not to see past his son's glazed look of arrogance and ignorance, and as his son stomped and annoyed folk, Arthur made excuses.

The library had had enough.

The Settlers were not big on meetings; on account of the women's "a penis is only the beginning" placard incident, rarely did more than two meet. Today was different: Arthur of the North was staring at the Librarian *and* a reader.

They were not budging.

"He stomps about like he owns the place, like he lives here, pays the rent, and feeds us," said the Librarian.

"I can assure you he doesn't feed me," muttered the reader.

"This place is not the place for stomping," muttered the Librarian, who lived for silence.

Arthur of the North thought of his large son. He was handsome in an apelike way, with massive hands, long hair, a full set of teeth, and a voice that purred. He could read a shopping list and have women sighing.

"But he's a giant," said Arthur of the North. "He can't help it; his tiptoeing makes the noise of a bass drum."

"That man has never tiptoed," said the reader.

"And what about the balance for overdue books?" said the Librarian. "He laughed in my face the last time I mentioned it."

Arthur of the North pulled out his payment book. "How much?"

"It is not for you to pay; he's a grown man," muttered the Librarian.

The reader tutted. "And where is this *giant* now? Why is he not here instead of you?"

Arthur of the North said nothing.

"Strutting I suppose," said the reader.

"Women welcome his strutting," muttered Arthur of the North. "I have never seen them so happy."

"What would a woman know?" said the Librarian.

The reader nodded.

Arthur of the North thought of his mother and sighed. She knew every pickling thing, and she knew it before anyone else.

"Some women dream of your son's seed and what it would produce," she'd said, "and it's gone to his head. He will soon be uncontrollable."

Was she right? Was he uncontrollable now?

"I think he's mending ropes," muttered Arthur of the North, "for the next Arrival Day."

"But that's six months from now," said the Librarian.

Arthur of the North sighed. "Apparently, there is a lot of drying involved."

The reader threw a look at the Librarian.

"Yes, well, waiting, it seems, is all you do with that son of yours," said the reader.

He stopped.

A woman crashed through the library entrance.

The reader caught a glimpse of a skirt and, with a sharp intake of breath, swore.

The Librarian, embracing his authority, stood and was about shout, then caught the look in Aggie's eye.

The two men turned to Arthur; his face fell.

"Let's call it a day," said the Librarian.

"Yes," muttered the reader.

Without a word, Arthur of the North followed Aggie back to his mother for the laying of hemp on the dead's eyes.

Arthur of the North, now a man in his sixties, had long forgotten how to cry. His face was a blank mask, despite his heart breaking; coming to terms with a life without his mother with something he dreaded.

For sixty years, he had lived under the strong arm of his mother. Now, he had to do it not only alone but with James the Strong chipping at his heels and bollocking everything up.

He went through the cremation preparations and, with the help of Aggie, organized the raising of Wife-ie's obelisk to catch the morning sun.

Aggie had nowhere to go; the women viewed her as a "two-faced suck-up" who couldn't be trusted with a hemp teabag let alone to help with the nurturing of things.

They, with a healthy suspicion for Wife-ie and all who belonged to her, slammed the door in Aggie's face.

"Go lick some other pickling arse," shouted one.

"Yeah!" shouted another.

It was the treaties that did it, and of course the hemp.

Every time the baby quota was full, Wife-ie created more treaties, calling them "a mere box-ticking exercise."

In the good ol' days, Wife-ie approached at hemp-picking time when the women, high and happy, didn't even see the small print let alone read it. Several treaties later, the quotas had changed, expanded, and finally been rubbed out, along with most of the women's rights, until the day hemp-nurturing was taken from the women.

Wife-ie approached with her usual smugness, asking a bunch of hempless and sober women to sign the latest treaty.

The treaty was anything but a box-ticking exercise; it was an enslavement contract.

"We're buggered," said the woman who looked like a horse.

The women demanded a viewing of all treaties.

"Burnt," said Wife-ie. "Security—you can never trust these Aliens."

What the Aliens had to do with treaties, the women had no idea, but they knew Wife-ie was lying: she was meticulous when it came to papers and reading. Her burning a treaty was as believable as her having a heart.

"You're a woman like us," they said. "You should be on our side."

Wife-ie, as immovable as her soon-to-be-erected obelisk, threw them a cold look.

"Think of your sons," she said. "The less you have, the more for them."

Aggie and Arthur of the North sat by Wife-ie's body, prepared and cleaned for "the burning," as a fire was building outside.

"Never settle for one partner, that's what Mother said. Now look at me—alone." He turned to Aggie. "How will I know a good decision from a bad one?"

"What about your advisers?" said Aggie.

"Them—they want my son tossed to the Aliens." He looked at Aggie. "He has no offspring; his seed is as barren as the planet we left. In fact, some want to send him there."

Aggie said nothing; she had yet to meet this James the Strong.

James the Strong loved hanging out in the nurturing shed to bathe and dance with the women before sex. In fact, he had turned baby-making back to the good old days when it was fun; however, there was no offspring.

Wife-ie called it *early menopause*, something celebrated by women and never mentioned by men.

"James the Strong's long hair's a dead giveaway," said Wife-ie, and no one argued.

Fertile men were bald by the time they were thirty and wore wigs, which everyone knew but rarely mentioned; *wig* was a dirty word in the city.

No baby made James the Strong depressed and angry, leading to stomping in the library, which didn't have one book let alone a leaflet about infertility.

"All the others have 'em," he said to his father, "even those pickling Foreigners. What do I have? A poxy four-legged creature to toss a stick at."

His father told him to calm down. "All that stomping will make you limp," he lied. He, like most men, had no idea about infertility.

"Maybe he just needs to try a more fertile woman," said Aggie with absolutely no faith in what she said.

Arthur of the North patted her knee and thanked her for her kindness.

Then Aggie did the only thing she knew how to do—stroke—and for the first time, it led to more than a coughing fit.

Chapter Eight

AGGIE

"Not all mirrors show the same thing."—The Librarian

*A*ggie stared at her reflection in a pool. She rarely saw her face; she had been warned against it.

"Never look in a pool of water," said Wife-ie. "It's impossible to see yourself the same again."

Aggie looked at her slim features, her smooth skin—nothing like Arthur of the North's wrinkles she had stared at in bed an hour ago.

She sighed . . .

Wrinkles after great sex were lines that hypnotized, that were traced with a lover's finger and kissed. She had kissed every wrinkle on Arthur of the North's forehead, neck, and lower bits, and her body was singing with the pleasure of it . . .

She had never kissed before, let alone anything else. She wondered if this was what they did at the nurturing shed, just as she wondered if there would be a next time . . .

Arthur of the North offered to take her back to the nurturing shed. He was a gentleman at heart, and when she told him the door was closed, he, perturbed, looked at the sweet face of Aggie. There were no plans for what would happen after Wife-ie's burial, apart from—perhaps—celebrating.

He smiled at her. "Why don't you take over Mother's post?" he said. "Those library idiots have it in for my son, but you—you could keep them on their toes." His face lit up. "I could visit, better than that nurturing shed. Sometimes I feel like they're just going through the motions."

He traced his finger on her smooth skin. "Not like you."

Aggie moved into Wife-ie's room and became the new Wife-ie, her many talents springing to life like a disturbed rattlesnake.

Aggie had many talents; she could memorize a formula at a glance, design like there was no tomorrow, and have a redundant penis as pert as a pubescent bull. She had the vision of a genius, the hand of a prostitute, and the determination of a bull in heat.

She, in her first of many "I'll think for myself" moments, took the Library's archaic, out-of-date, long-winded, no-one-can-find-a-thing "filing" and developed two systems: a complex rabbit warren to hide Wife-ie's memoirs, treaties, and any other secrets from the public, and for the public shelves . . .

Shelves filled with readings, leaflets, and pictures, lit up so anyone could see right away what they were looking for. Shelves full of promise, stories, and recipes that made even the toothless drool.

Aggie understood other people's secrets like she was born to it, and people like she could read their minds. Whether it was the years spent with Wife-ie, she had no idea, but her brain buzzed like the electric dashboard of the sewage system.

"People need mystery, myths, and knowledge, fake or real," she said to the Librarian, who was happy to agree with her despite her being a woman.

In her spare time, Aggie practiced Wife-ie's stretching-and-posing-with-breathing techniques. The "Wife-ie techniques," as Aggie called them, not only cleanse the innards but keep a woman fresh well past her sell-by date.

The women poo-hooed Wife-ie's techniques.

"Anything that comes from that old bird's mouth is dirt fertilizer," shouted the horselike woman.

No one argued, until, five years down the line, Aggie began to defy age.

James the Strong was the first to notice. He was strutting through the library looking for policies on baby-snatching when he came across Aggie mid tree pose in the filing room.

He watched as she bent forward, breathed in, sighed out, and then stretched into a catlike position.

Her face glowed, and for the first time, he could see what it was his father saw in her . . .

He strutted into the small cubbyhole of a room—lit by a candle.

"What is all this then?" he grunted.

"It's good for trapped wind," she said.

He stopped. "Wind? A woman has wind?"

"Of course," she said.

"They told me that was just great sex," he said.

Aggie moved into a tree pose. She didn't have the heart to tell him women lied when it came to things in bed.

"Well, I'm not in bed, now am I?" She squeaked a small fart.

James the Strong chuckled.

Aggie caught a look—an Arthur of the North look—and smiled to herself.

Always the simple things with men, she thought.

As James the Strong, with one puff, blew out her candle.

Chapter Nine

APPETITES

"A good bed dive is worth a thousand words."–James the Strong

Five years on

*A*ggie looked at the blank face of James the Strong. He was staring at the ceiling like he always did after a decent night's shagging.

James the Strong's appetite, like his father's, was huge, but it was so different, a much more robust form of thrusting. The sort that had Aggie yelling like a banshee taming a wild horse, which for some reason spurred James the Strong on, like a wild horse with a whip.

In fact, she often used one.

Five years bouncing from father to son like a ping pong ball in a tornado was not how Aggie had planned her life. Remembering the names, their little ways, could tax even the finest memory, and father and son were as different as soya and hemp, but she had managed it, giving her a life she for the most part enjoyed, apart from James the Strong and his "I want a son" rants.

He turned to her. "What I wouldn't give for a son."

She sighed. How many times?

"I'm pushing forty with nothing to prove," said James the Strong.

Here we go . . .

"I've even shagged an Alien."

"Must we?" muttered Aggie.

She sighed, pulled back the covers, and headed for the bathroom as James the Strong regaled her with his story *yet again.*

"I dressed as a woman." He smiled to himself. "Took the swaps to the point, a nice cozy armchair and hammers from what I remember—no one had a clue it was me." James the Strong almost laughed.

Aggie sat on the john and pulled the toilet paper with disgust.

For five years they had been together, and she had heard the Alien story so many times she could repeat it word for word—backwards.

"Was your one-handed swinging of the armchair not a giveaway?" she said with a tired expression.

"You would think," said James the Strong. He looked at his nails. "But no"—he smiled to himself—"there I was by the field as instructed, and there she was, a sunburnt Alien waiting with a bag of soya and some apples. She didn't know what hit her."

"I can imagine." Aggie flushed the john.

"She laughed," said James the Strong.

"Imagine laughing at you," said Aggie.

James the Strong watched Aggie emerge from the bathroom.

"Loved the licking," he said.

"Did she?" Aggie sighed.

"I told her it was my trademark."

"Probably not something to brag about," Aggie muttered.

"No baby, though," he sighed, "and I heard those Aliens breed like rabbits."

"I wouldn't believe all you hear," said Aggie.

He watched her slide on her dressing gown and sit beside him.

Aggie traced a line around his nipple and looked at his irresistible eyes. *If only he didn't speak.*

"Why can't you be happy like your father?" she said.

"Happy? How can I be happy? I want a son. All the others have a son, why can't I? They have a son to walk with, talk with—what have I got? More four-legged creatures you can shake a stick at."

"They do return them to you." Aggie sighed.

"So what," mumbled James the Strong. "I want a son to mold."

She looked at him.

"Or at least show things to."

Aggie looked at her watch.

"Like how to pull a spaceship, the trick to tying it to one's back . . ."

"There's a trick?" said Aggie. "You never said anything about a trick."

He stopped. "Yes, well, we all have our secrets . . ."

"It's just tying though, isn't it?" said Aggie.

"There's tying and then there's tying," he muttered.

Aggie looked at him like he was talking twaddle.

"And then there's the drying of the rope."

"Now you're being silly," said Aggie.

"A secret I'll take to my grave." He stopped and slid his hand onto Aggie's breast. "If there's no son to leave it to."

Aggie pushed the hand away.

"You're always banging on about a son. What about a daughter? I'm sure there are plenty of girls who'd love to know about rope . . . drying?"

"Pfff," he said. "A daughter—for men to fill with their seed?"

She looked at him. "That's what you do to me."

"But that's different," he said.

"How?" she said.

"Well, you're one of them," said James the Strong.

Aggie sighed.

"You know, a woman who pleases," he said, "who needs man's seed, and mine is, well . . . good for you . . ."

She threw him a "really?" look.

"It's like my name." He laughed.

"Strong?" said Aggie she stared at James the Strong's blank face. *Thank pickle we have no children,* she thought.

At the beginning, she thought about babies, but she had seen the worn-out looks of those at the nurturing shed and figured if they were worn out *without* James the Strong to interfere—or "mold," as he put it —then what would motherhood be like *with* him?

Could the planet take another *him*? Could *she* take another him?

Even though his sperm was as fertile as a scrambled egg, she took action. She saw it as her moral duty to end the James the Strong line before it got started—it was the least she could do for all the benefits she enjoyed with her position.

Contraception was banned on Planet Hy Man, the formula hidden, and yet it was so simple even James the Strong could follow it . . .

Aggie, having sorted the secret files into her rabbit warren, knew all about the formula: no sex during a full moon and using a sponge type thing "down there"— which, in the end, was Aggie's downfall.

After five years of illegal family planning, watching, avoiding, and being prepared, Aggie, thanks to a night of way too much hemp, threw caution to the wind.

It was the end of the arrival of the Aliens' celebration day—celebrated by all bar the Aliens.

During the yearly celebration, the whole city closed as men and women reenacted the day of running the Aliens out of town by chasing, feasting, and catching, usually in dark corners for ravaging.

Aggie had vague memories of watching from her window with several hemp smokes and a bucket of home brew; drunk, stoned, and singing, she thought, *Bugger the sponge thingy* and dived onto the bed with Arthur of the North.

It was all a bit of a blur . . .

Did James the Strong visit after that?

She couldn't remember.

A week later, she woke up, raced to the john, and threw up the previous night's spicy tofu.

"Was it that bad?" yelled James the Strong.

"What?" Aggie gurgled through a gag.

"My cooking."

She looked up, wiped her mouth, and wondered, *How stupid can a man be?*

"Did you visit after the celebrations the other night?" she asked as casually as possible.

"Celebration . . . night?" muttered James the Strong.

"Yes . . . for some bed-diving?"

"Hmmm, don't recall," he said.

"Shit," muttered Aggie. She stared into the toilet bowl.

It had never been her plan to sleep with anyone, but when the nurturing shed door closed and Arthur of the North lurched, she saw an opening. Now, all these years later, she had a baby inside her . . . and the father was probably not the right one.

"Shit, shit, shit."

"What was that, luv?" said James the Strong.

"Shit and bollocks."

"If you fancy a spot of bed-diving, I've got five minutes . . ."

The next day, Aggie picked her moment. After some gentle snogging in the sun, Arthur of the North closed his eyes, and she told him.

He slid his hand onto her stomach as his old tired face smiled.

"If he looks like my James, you're laughing," said Arthur of the North.

Chapter Ten

OFFSPRING

"A woman's limit is all in her mind."–Fanny

*A*ggie swore. She was in the library, attempting a yoga tree pose while trying not to throw up.

She felt trapped, scared—in fact, terrified. Arthur of the North seemed to think she had the brains to pull off a paternity lie; she, however, had doubts. James the Strong was, well, strong and vengeful . . .

She stumbled.

"Oh, great pickling sperm," she shouted.

The Librarian, with a skid, stopped at the doorway. "Ma'am?"

She glared at him. "Must you call me 'ma'am'?"

"Apologies, ma'am."

Aggie clutched her mouth and gagged.

The Librarian said nothing. He'd read enough to know morning sickness when he saw it, and he saw enough to know who the father was.

"The trick is to sleep with two simultaneously," he said.

"What?" Aggie gulped.

"That's what Wife-ie says. 'Sleep with the enemy, sleep with your friend, and never let the right hand know what the left is doing.'" He pulled one of Wife-ie's memoirs from a shelf and slid it toward Aggie. "You should read it. It might help."

Aggie looked at him with a "why are you helping me?" look.

She and the Librarian had a "let's put up with each other" sort of relationship. Him helping her was as plausible as James the Strong completing a crossword.

Aggie suspected the Librarian knew why she spent so much time in the rabbit warren. It was the way he sniffed as she entered and muttered "satisfied?" when she left. The way he, despite a Do not Disturb sign, walked in on her plotting the moons and carving up sponges with a "Feeling artistic today, are we, ma'am?"

He even collected sponges for her . . . helped her hack out a few "small enough to fit 'whatever,'" like he knew nothing of contraception.

Arthur of the North told her not to worry, that the Librarian was just a "queer sort of fella," the sort who "never ventured near the nurturing shed except to pick up wig tips."

Aggie looked at his outrageous wig, *perched* like a Persian cat with piles. *It says a lot about him,* she thought.

"It's all about doing your bit for the planet." He pointed to the book.

"We all do our bit," snapped Aggie.

"You've done more than many—mostly on your back," said the Librarian.

She threw him a glare.

"You've kept James the Strong out of the nutrient shed, and the men are truly grateful. I mean before you came along, there was a waiting list."

"Glad to be of service." She straightened herself and, with a decisive gulp, resumed her pose.

The Librarian eyed her belly. Without thinking, she touched it.

"The future of the planet is tentative," he said. "Poised like a four-legged creature on the tip of a needle, as precarious as the outlands."

"The outlands are hardly precarious. We send the women there."

She stopped, thinking of James the Strong.

"Well . . . mostly."

The Librarian smiled like he knew what she was thinking. Then he waited until the silence was uncomfortable.

Aggie squeaked a small fart.

"Pardon," she muttered.

"Now is biggest moment of your life, ma'am," said the Librarian.

She stopped. "What?"

"Every step you take is . . . well . . . crucial."

Silence.

"You need to steer with clarity," he said.

Aggie glared at the Librarian. Him making sense was as rare as contraception.

"Must we always talk of clarity? Every time you mention that word I leave as confused as James the Strong with his tax return."

A lump was forming in her throat; it was going nowhere but up. She attempted a gulp.

The Librarian handed her a glass of water—the perfect temperature. She tried a sip . . . just as James the Strong arrived, panting with distress.

"It's Father," he said. "You need to come. I don't know what to do. He's delirious, talking of-diving on beds and off springs."

The Librarian threw Aggie a look followed by a "my lips are zipped" gesture, which James the Strong assumed was something men in stupid wigs always did.

Aggie was by Arthur of the North's bedside in minutes, holding his hand as he gasped for breath. James the Strong stood outside; watching someone die was woman's work.

Aggie looked at the familiar face of her only true friend.

"You're not old enough to go," she whispered.

"Wasps know nothing of age," he said, "and when one stings, there's nothing you can do."

A tear rolled down her cheek.

You have made me so happy, she thought.

"We had our moments." He smiled and patted her cheek.

"More than moments . . . a lifetime," she said.

"I know," he said. "There are no words."

His eyes lit up as he stared to the heavens; he stretched out his hand, making as if to grab for something higher.

The medicine official looked at Aggie with a shrug. "Just the drugs, ma'am."

"I see it all now," Arthur of the North said.

"May be overdid the sedative," muttered the medicine official.

"It's so clear, it's perfect," said Arthur of the North.

The medicine official threw Aggie a look, then shouted, "what do you see? A light? An angel?"

"Bed-diving and babies." Arthur of the North smiled. "They're all at it." And then, with a cough, he stopped breathing.

The medicine official looked at Aggie. "Bed-diving[1]?"

"It's a figure of speech," muttered Aggie.

James the Strong, just as his father did, leaned on Aggie as she organized the funeral of the century. It was the sort of funeral that any Viking would have given their eyeteeth for. The sort never seen before on Planet Hy Man.

The bonfire was higher than any statue, built from unwanted furniture, wood, leftover food, and eggshells—the smell was not brilliant.

James did not account for the smell; he was too preoccupied with height, and as he was a giant himself, that meant pretty high.

It took three days for the bonfire to burn to waist height and three more to cool down enough to spread across fields, hen coops, and the odd hidden hemp plant.

It was a magnificent night, and as the father of Aggie's son went up in flames, the son fluttered about Aggie's womb almost like he knew.

Aggie watched the celebrating crowd from the balcony with James the Strong beside her.

The women had been let loose to dance and tantalize. Apart from celebrating days, women spent their time in the nurturing sheds[2] and used a booking system for baby-making: Arthur of the North's suggestion, care of Aggie, not that anyone knew—apart from the Librarian.

With Arthur of the North now a pile of ash and the booking system thrown to the wind, the men soon threw themselves into fighting and rolling about on the ground, relishing the chance to impress a woman, while some women began to regret their frenzied dancing.

To many men, the booking system was on par with a visit to the dentist, and the idea of being chosen rather than making a booking went to their heads. So engrossed in impressing, the men often didn't notice when a woman, bored and fed up, moved on.

Some women made a quick retreat, others made a mental note to avoid future *death* celebrations, while others, carried away, cheered like wild banshees at a cockfight.

The mixed messages confused the men. It had been ages since they'd had to read body language, interpret a woman's "no." It didn't take long for some to crumble, unable to cope when rejected, lost to another male, especially when punched in the face.

Aggie watched; she had never seen anything like it before. "Arthur of the North would have a fit of the hairies," she said.

James the Strong laughed. "The fighting is all playacting. The whole rape-and-pillage thing is more a ceremony than anything." He laughed again. "Swapping and swinging." He eyed Aggie's belly with a sigh. "Reminds me of the good ol' days."

Aggie watched as a bull-like Foreigner punched a weedy man to the ground, tossed his wig to the wind, lifted a woman over his shoulders, and disappeared into the dark with a "let's be having yer!" shout.

"Why does everything have to led to ravaging," muttered Aggie.

"It's because they don't have you," said James the Strong. "That was me until I met you."

She watched the wigless man as he jumped to his feet, scrabbled for his wig, and ran like a stunned chicken toward the nurturing shed.

"Really?" she muttered.

"The number of women I've tossed over my shoulder," muttered James the Strong. He eyed Aggie. "You fancy a toss?"

Aggie didn't hear.

She was too busy watching the crowd descend into a rabble, the words of the Librarian haunting her.

Did the planet really balance like a whatever on a needle?

Cryptic, she thought. Why so pickling cryptic?

---

1. *An act that requires neither beds nor the art of diving.*
2. *The tools of a nurturing shed are kept hidden from all until needed, once seen, a woman rarely opens her legs again.*

Chapter Eleven

CHOICES

"All women need limits, but men are limitless."–James the Strong

*A*ggie told herself a baby would be the making of James the Strong, that he would burst forth from the shadows of his father and become the man she thought he should be . . . and when she didn't believe that, she told herself she could manipulate with a little bed-diving.

The truth was, she didn't have much choice.

James the Strong followed her about like one of those four-legged creatures who followed him about. But, unlike James the Strong, she didn't toss sticks for him to fetch; she silently put up with him, unsure of what to do, what Arthur of the North would have her do.

Arthur of the North had embraced Aggie and James the Strong's relationship, forever telling her that she would be the making of his son.

She was still waiting . . .

She never did believe Arthur of the North, but she didn't argue, because when James the Strong shut his mouth, he was delicious to be with. And at least she knew where she stood, she told herself, *not like those in the shed.*

And if James the Strong knew about his father and Aggie, he never let on. He assumed a night with him was enough to keep a woman, that Aggie would never look at another again. Besides, his father had loved the idea of him and Aggie. "You need a younger man," he said. "Just like him."

It was like he had thrown them together, like clay on a potter's wheel swirling around for molding . . .

Into what, Aggie had no idea.

After the funeral and several days of emptying the city of its home brew and hemp supplies, James the Strong stared out into the mess of the courtyard. Sipping his hemp tea, he watched the dawn sun rise on a courtyard strewn with paper plates, crushed cups, and piles of hemp dog-ends.

His father would have controlled the celebrations better; at least have the punters tidy up.

Suddenly it hit him, what a great leader his father was; he had never noticed, let alone told him. He was too busy fooling around, annoying the Librarian, chasing skirt. He was so far up his own arse he never saw the work his father did. All he'd done was take the love of his father's life from him, just because he could.

Shame slapped him like a wet fish around the face, then doubt followed; how could he carry on?

He watched as people began to trickle into the courtyard looking for leadership.

What do they want?

He drained his tea . . . then retired to his room, pulled the curtains across the magnificent waterfall view, slumped on his bed, and cried.

The Librarian, with a box of recycled tissues, didn't even knock. He burst in, shoved the box under James the Strong's nose, and told him, "Pull your royal arse together."

James the Strong, a little confused about the arse-pulling, blew his nose, the noise trumpeting through the corridors as loud as his tiptoeing.

"You're all that they have." The Librarian gestured to the now-chanting masses.

James the Strong sniffed.

"It may not be much . . ." said the Librarian.

"What do you mean 'much'?" James the Strong glared.

"But it is what it is." The Librarian sighed with camp drama.

"And what is that?" huffed James the Strong. He blew his nose again; the tissue buckled under the volume.

"A people ready to be led, a city ready to expand, make things, taxes to spend," said the Librarian. "Your father left you a lot."

"What am I to do with it?" James the Strong looked at his soaked tissue. "Me, a man that pulls spaceships and gets four-legged creatures to fetch?"

The Librarian handed him a fresh tissue. "It's a start."

"Start? My father made it look so easy, I'm shaking in my boots," said James the Strong.

"First thing you need to do is some addressing."

"Oh?" said James the Strong.

"A speech about your father," said the Librarian.

"Arrrrh, yes—that's what Aggie said. "She made one, said I could use it."

"How sweet," muttered the Librarian, who had also written one.

"The next is perhaps get rid of her."

James the Strong jumped. "Get rid of her? I can't get rid of her. She's the only thing I want—no, need. I can't make . . . do . . . anything. She is my rock, my waterfall, my pouch of hemp, my—"

"Or . . ." the Librarian interrupted.

"What?" said James the Strong.

"Change her status," he said with a look of distaste.

"She? A woman? There is no status . . . well, except to keep me happy, and perhaps a little filing in the library."

"Bit more than that," muttered the Librarian.

"Well yes, but a woman is but a uterus for seed."

"That sort of talk will get you thrown to the outlands," muttered the Librarian.

Won't mind, thought James the Strong, thinking of the sunburnt Alien.

"And she *is* carrying your child," said the Librarian.

"Oh yes, forgot about that. Need to hang around, I suppose." James the Strong stared at his tissue wondering just how flimsy a piece of hemp could be.

"Suppose?" snapped the Librarian. "For years you have been banging on about a child—"

"Have I?" said James the Strong. He tossed his tissue at the bin and watched it hit its mark.

"Yes, like that waterfall out your window. You've never stopped."

"Oh." James the Strong stopped. "Should you be talking to me like this?"

"Well, someone has to."

"That's what Aggie says," muttered James the Strong.

James the Strong stood on the balcony overlooking the waterfall and pulled out Aggie's speech. He had read it so many times he could recite it if it wasn't for his nerves.

Aggie waited in the wings until James the Strong pulled her beside him and slid his arm into hers.

The crowd hushed; a woman so flagrantly branded like a prized four-legged creature was unheard of.

She thought about pushing away, until James the Strong slid his other hand on her belly and she caught the Librarian's eye.

She didn't move but forced a smile, thanking the gods of the galaxies that she had put a decent dress on. James the Strong talked of his father and the crowd listened.

James the Strong, under the guidance of Aggie, had organized drummers and food, and as the crowd—hungover and hungry—moved towards the food, he turned to Aggie.

Over the few days following his father's death, he had thought of many things, some which made his head hurt, but thanks to the Librarian, he had come to one conclusion.

If he didn't have Aggie on his side, someone else would, and that someone would take over what he had. Not that he didn't dream of running away, but over the last few days, he had watched the masses and realized being one of them would be worse than trying to tame a wild horse with only a set of piles for company.

He turned to Aggie. "I don't want to share you," he said. "I want you all to myself."

Aggie was silent.

"And I was thinking, now I am, well, in my father's footsteps, I could make changes."

That wig-wearing knob of a Librarian was right, she thought.

"You watch, James the Strong will change," he'd said. "He'll want to leave his own stamp on things, and you'll need to use all your bed-diving powers to keep him in tow—not make a mess of things."

Aggie looked into the hard and black eyes of the giant.

"I want you and my son beside me," he muttered.

She thought of her son. *His legacy.*

James the Strong gestured for the band to stop. The crowd looked up . . .

"No more quotas, no more nurturing shed—as my Aggie says, 'the times they are a-changing.'"

"What?" said Aggie.

The crowd looked from one to the other, confused. *Aggie?*

"There is more than one way to build a city, and I have found mine," said James the Strong.

With great ceremony, he unraveled the Librarian's speech to read.

"We need to treasure our women, stop all this appointment business," he pronounced.

The crowd muttered and murmured, some in panic.

"Does that mean no sex?" shouted a voice from the back.

"Segregation?" shouted another.

James the Strong looked about his "flock," as he had taken to calling them, and tightened his grip on Aggie.

"This is my Aggie, who I own, take care of, feed, and . . . make babies with. And I invite all you men to do the same—choose a woman to care for."

The crowd hushed; the men and women looked at each other. *Were they to cheer?*

Chapter Twelve

THE OWNERSHIP ACT

"Freedom without education is but a poisoned chalice."—Fanny

*T*he crowd were confused. No one had talked of caring so publicly before. In fact, most men had no idea what it meant.

"Well at least we'll know where we stand," muttered a woman from the back.

"Stand—we'll hardly be standing, we'll be on our backs," said the horselike woman.

"So nothing has changed then," muttered another woman.

"I don't know," said a jack-of-all-trades.

"Let's become the civilization we were meant to be!" yelled James the Strong.

"And what's that?" yelled a voice from the back.

"Education," Aggie whispered to James the Strong, "with order and the vulnerable protected."

"Lots of ordering," yelled James the Strong.

"Ordering?" yelled a voice from the back.

The crowd, even more confused, began to murmur.

"Ordering what?"

"Yeah, from where?"

"I said 'order,'" whispered Aggie.

"Order, not ordering," yelled James the Strong.

"And education," whispered Aggie.

Soon a woman being owned by a man was all the rage, the "in" thing. Then it became law, and the nurturing shed was closed for reconstruction.

Under Aggie's suggestion, the nurturing shed, having a fair amount of equipment for birthing and the like, seemed a good place to expand into an institute for scientific learning. Starting, as Aggie suggested, with a way of protecting people from wasps—"perhaps something that involves needles?"

James the Strong loved the idea. Wasps plagued the city, and when he saw the crowd cheering, he felt a surge of pleasure he had never felt before. He wanted more cheering; he wanted to walk out on the balcony every day and face that applause, and he offered to fund the institute himself.

"I will give up a few things," he shouted, though *not quite sure what,* and the crowd cheered.

Six months later, James the Strong, sprawled out on his king-size bed, pondered his new life and the joy of being *liked.*

His favorite bit was the speech-reading; he loved it, *all that standing on the balcony and yelling.*

And he was built for it, not like his father, who had to stand on a stool and have someone hold up a placard of what he was saying.

James the Strong's voice purred, ricocheting around the courtyard like a moth in a lampshade. Even the Aliens could hear the odd word, on a calm day.

It was all in the design of the courtyard—a design courtesy of Aggie—and, of course, the voice-vibrator.

In the past, men hated him, but not now; he had given a whole woman to each, forever. The only thing a man had to do was pick . . .

Under the new ownership act[1], a woman could swoon and flirt all she liked, but once owned by a man, she was his to dive on, talk at, and feed.

With one act, James the Strong had become a "man's man." He had given men so much and women even less.

Each day he was greeted with cheers, backslaps, and handshakes from the men and little from women.

Life had changed drastically for women. Not only were they to make babies, but they had to catch a man first.

They still couldn't earn a living or learn things or even own a place. Instead, they were shuffled off to the huts the Foreigners had left for the art corner and, with an "it's only temporary" promise, tried to make the best of things.

Free to roam with the sole aim of attracting a man, they started talking of good and bad catches and ways to attract, some getting a little up themselves when they had a choice.

Others, like Fanny, yearned for the good old days.

Fanny, claimed by an opulent Settler, was one of the first to be owned.

"A bad shag is for life now," she said, "and what's worse, there is no complaints department."

James the Strong slid his arm behind his head and watched his Aggie undress.

She slipped off her shoe . . .

"This leading thing is not as bad as I first thought," he said.

She slipped off her stockings.

He sighed.

Her dress fell to the ground, her hair to her shoulders . . . then finally her bra . . .

In the moonlight, she always took his breath away—stopped him talking.

"How 'bout some bed-diving," he purred, and then, forgetting about how bed-diving worked, grabbed his Aggie and pulled her to him.

Over the next few months, James the Strong watched his Aggie expand with child, often wondering how he would have done any of "this leading thing" without her. And as her tummy grew, he marveled at it, touching it, always with his ear pressed to her stomach, listening to the baby.

For the first time in his life, James the Strong was truly happy, so happy he was willing to try any shagging position to work around the bump—even give up bed-diving—until the offspring was born.

Aggie began to relax, enjoy her status, and make plans for her son, collecting information in the library.

Until Aggie's son Manifesto the Great was born; then things changed. For a start, James the Strong was not crazy about the name.

---

1. The sort of marriage most civilisations were built on.

Chapter Thirteen

MANIFESTO THE GREAT

"Coming too late is not as glamorous as many make out."—The
captain of the third spaceship

Ten years on

*W*hen Manifesto the Great was born, the crowd cheered, celebrated, even talked of a new world.

James the Strong looked down at the pink bundle and expected to feel the same, but the only thing he felt was a mild repulsion, and when Aggie bent to feed him, James the Strong left the room to throw up.

Manifesto the Great was a long string of a baby who had the promise of height until the age of ten, when, like Arthur of the North, all growth stopped.

Aggie watched him mature with her heart in her mouth. Each day he looked more like his father, Arthur of the North, and she missed him so much . . .

What she wouldn't give to sit under the sun, hold his hand, inhale the delicious scent of his hair, and talk . . .

James the Strong had no idea about proper talk or how to make her laugh.

In the early days, it didn't matter. Making love was easy—it was all looks and sighs. James the Strong stopped talking at the mere flick of a shoe. Not now; he talked and never stopped, and it was the sort of talk that dried up every orifice in her body. When he opened his mouth, she just wanted to shut it again, but nothing would shut him up.

She could toss her bra out the window, swing from their bedroom chandelier naked, her family jewels pert and pristine like a sunflower, and he would still talk. If only he had the mouth of his father, a man that made her laugh and think . . .

She sighed.

What a waste, she thought, of a spectacular family member.

When the missing overwhelmed her, Aggie went to her secret drawer in the old room, the room where she'd stayed while caring for Wife-ie. No one went to that damp hole of a place. James the Strong even threatened to grow potatoes in it, and when Aggie protested way too much, he sent the Librarian to find out why.

The Librarian caught her with his usual feigning-an-emergency act, bursting in for a surprise effect (an entrance he was famous for and probably why most disliked him).

Aggie, with her back to him, was bent over an opened drawer, clutching a pair of old underpants.

She sniffed.

A tear dropped to the floor.

The door slammed shut.

Aggie, mid inhale, jolted and then turned, boxers swinging from her hand—nothing like the sort seen hanging out on the washing line.

"I recognize them," said the Librarian.

He moved closer. "So old-fashioned."

He spied the "my Arthur" embroidered on the crotch.

Aggie covered it with her fingers.

"Don't tell," she whispered.

The Librarian stared at the ancient boxers that used to swing from the leader's laundry.

Aggie looked at him. "It's all I have of him."

The Librarian moved closer, made to touch the boxers, and stopped. For a moment he inhaled, lost in thought. "Hemp, after so many years, still holds it shape," he whispered.

"Nothing but the best for Arthur." She sighed.

"Nothing but the best," muttered the Librarian.

She fingered the crotch, then folded it and placed it tenderly back in the drawer.

"*He* never wears underwear," she said.

The Librarian jolted. "Who?"

"Who do you think?"

"Pfff, him—everyone knows about the leader airing his family member," said the Librarian.

"Real men swing, according to him," said Aggie.

"There is merit in that theory—so I've heard," said Librarian.

"But not standing on a balcony in a leader's toga." Aggie caught his eye.

"Quite," said the Librarian. "The masses talk of an eyeful and James the Strong in the same breath . . ."

He eyed Aggie.

"Not quite leadership material."

He flashed a smile that stopped at the corners of his mouth.

"Your secret is safe with me."

Aggie knew that look. Nothing was safe with it, especially secrets . . .

The Librarian knew which side his hemp was rolled on. They were living in exciting times—the city was expanding, they were building a better world, and Aggie, despite being a woman, made it all possible. *She* had a brain; solving problems and dealing with complaints was a breeze with her.

All he had to do was bide his time and wait for her to slip up, and the library would be *his* pleasure dome and James the Strong *his* leader.

The Librarian reassured James the Strong with one of his cryptic looks. And James the Strong, preoccupied and "run off his feet," happily accepted the Librarian's word.

The truth was, without Aggie, James the Strong couldn't rule. The meetings confounded him, had him flopping onto his bed flummoxed with a spinning head. It was all that talking, information, *and* decision-making: he was expected to know everything and, in an instant, decide what to do.

It was Aggie who arranged all meetings to be held in the "action room" of the library where she could spy and listen. It was her idea to hold the meetings at night when the readers were tired and stuff them full of hemp biscuits and a nightcap, claiming that they would be "less likely to argue on a full stomach."

And it was her idea for James the Strong to "use your height, remain standing, and loom," as she put it.

He needed Aggie, despite the fact that she was more interested in her son than bed-diving and "must we" was now her usual response, but her rebuffs were wearing him down.

Ten years of watching your woman obsess over a son as foreign as, well, a Foreigner had taken its toll on James the Strong. It was not that he hated his child, but did Aggie have to talk about him *so* much, and did he have to look *so* like Arthur of the North and *so* unlike him?

Where were the big hands, the swagger?

Desperate and confused, he was starting to question himself. He couldn't understand why his son was not like him, why he was so . . . well . . . un-moldable, and whenever he asked Aggie, she'd clam up, pull a face.

She wouldn't even listen, let alone answer, and the more he asked, the more she withdrew.

As the years passed, his embarrassment smoldered, and when Aggie talked of separate bedrooms, his embarrassment turned to anger. He, the great leader, was turning into a figure of fun . . .

Chapter Fourteen

THE ART CENTRE

"Laying flowers at a statue's feet is woman's work. A man's is building them."—Loud Mouth

*T*he Art Centre kept itself separate from the city, allowing the four-legged creatures to roam, sniff, and roll in the grass, exposing their stomachs for a good rub. The four-legged creatures were loved and sometimes worshipped, making the Foreigners a joke to most in the city, including James the Strong.

He, like many in the city, celebrated everything with the burning of a four-legged creature followed by the peeling of flesh to eat and skins to decorate walls with.

The Foreigners preferred paint.

James the Strong loved the skins of the four-legged creatures so much he even had a pouch with long fluffy hair for his family member.

Not something Aggie liked to ponder on. It was all a bit meaty for her. She had tried to make the best of things over years, but no amount of cushions and color could camouflage the skins that hung in their bedroom.

When James the Strong didn't take the hint about separate bedrooms, she rehung his animal skins in his "sulking room," and when he still didn't take the hint, she moved in a bed and spent most evenings feigning a headache, a stomachache, or instigating an argument—sometimes all three.

After a particularly long meeting about the cost of statues, James the Strong, knackered with a spinning head of figures he could not comprehend, entered his bedroom.

He had heard rumors, rumors that in his heart he knew, and he was fed up.

Aggie, mid cushion fluffing, said nothing.

"Folk are talking," he said. "I hear their sniggers, and *quite frankly, it's embarrassing . . .*"

"Talking?" said Aggie without looking up.

"Our son, not being much like me."

"Don't be silly," said Aggie.

"He walks like he's tripping over something," said James the Strong.

Aggie tossed a cushion into the corner and picked up another.

"And his head's always in some sort of reading device; what's that about? I mean I tried to teach him how to pull a spaceship, but all Manifesto the so-called Great wanted to do was *play* in the pickling thing."

"He is only ten," said Aggie.

"But spaceship pulling is every boy's dream—it's our heritage," said James the Strong.

"Hardly heritage," muttered Aggie with an aggressive punch at a pillow.

She looked at him. "Maybe you should give up the spaceship pulling."

"Give up my birthright?" snapped James the Strong.

"Has it not been done to death?" said Aggie.

"Done to what?" said James the Strong.

"Have we not moved on?" said Aggie.

"How can you move on without a spaceship?" said James the Strong. "And they're still in good shape, bit like you . . ."

He eyed her, pondering a waist grab.

"Doesn't mean you have to drag them out every year, flog the whole arrival thing like a caveman."

James the Strong slumped on the bed. "Are you saying I'm a caveman?"

"Well, if the spacesuit fits," said Aggie.

"You used to like all my caveman stuff," sulked James the Strong.

He watched Aggie move about the bedroom. After ten years of ownership, he still yearned for her. She had aged well; he even told her once, and *did she appreciate it?*

Did she say 'thank you,' tell him he had?

"Bet you say that to all the girls" is what she said.

He peered down at his "out of action" family member, limp as a used tea bag under his "going to bed" toga. It, like the rest of him, was a giant, and, like the rest of him, had been a master in the bedroom, spouting forth in seconds like the great waterfall itself. Women used to go crazy for it, especially Aggie—she even dressed it up when "in the mood."

He sighed.

These days, there was as much chance of Aggie dressing up his family member as his so-called artistic son reaching for a rope to pull a ship.

James the Strong stared at his woman. Even a cuddle would help. *Is it too much to ask?*

He looked at Aggie with his best smile and patted the bed. "Why don't you come and sit down."

Aggie said nothing; she was engrossed in pillow fluffing, a habit she had taken to when James the Strong had his "fancy a toss over my shoulder" look. Pillow fluffing usually had him running to his sulking room.

She reached for another cushion, wondering how many it would take. He seemed planted on the bed, talking like no one had listened to him all day. She sighed. What she would give for some decent conversation . . . .

"Do you know what he called me the other day?" said James the Strong.

Aggie didn't answer.

"Daddy—*Daddy!*"

"What's wrong with that?" said Aggie. "Apparently, it's all the rage."

"Rage?" said James the Strong. "We are royalty. We don't follow rages, we make 'em."

"He *is* only ten," muttered Aggie.

"Ten? Ten?" snapped James the Strong.

"Yes, ten," said Aggie. "What were you doing at that age, picking your nose or just your bum?"

"Well, I certainly wasn't an arty-farty picklehead," snapped James the Strong.

Aggie grabbed another pillow.

"It's like living in the Art Centre with him, and what's all this 'abstract' bollocks? What ten-year-old talks of 'abstract'?"

Aggie let out a *here we go* sigh.

"I mean he pulls things apart, puts them back together."

"It's called recycling," snapped Aggie.

"Recycling's boring," huffed James the Strong. "Why doesn't he go and join the Foreigners and their so-called arts corner? Them and their 'save the four-legged creatures' sewage talk."

Aggie tossed the cushion into the corner and picked up another.

"He'll be making statues next," snapped James the Strong. "And it's not like we don't have enough of them. I mean how many statues does a city need?"

Aggie sighed.

"*And* they're all covered in flowers—a walk down the main street gives me a headache. I nearly passed out the other day."

Aggie pulled a face.

"*And . . . t*here's not even one of *me*—not one!"

"I wonder why," muttered Aggie.

"I mean I *am* the leader. You'd think there would at least be a head —somewhere."

"Well, there has always been the problem of your height and materials," said Aggie. "I mean your nose alone would take up half the road's budget."

"Well excuse me for breathing," huffed James the Strong.

He patted the bed again.

Aggie fluffed with vigor.

He looked at the walls. *He missed his skins.*

"You should be proud," said Aggie. "Manifesto the Great has been assigned."

"Assigned? You sound like one of those leaflets the readers like to print," he muttered, "for the masses."

"Our son's been assigned his own corner of creation."

James the Strong scowled.

"Our son?" Memories of the sniggers flooded back. "He's more like you than me."

Aggie stopped.

"That's just because he's ten—he's not a man."

"So you say," snapped James the Strong.

"He did give you that reflector," said Aggie.

James the Strong flicked his hair, rolled onto his side, and jumped out of bed; beating Aggie verbally was as easy as trying to understand one of her formulas, especially when she mentioned that *damnable reflector,* which, thanks to his son, had "taken the city by storm."

"Yes, well, thanks to those reflectors[1], no one has time for anything anymore but looking at themselves," he snapped, and with a slam of the door, he huffed to his sulking room—a place, it seemed, he was destined to spend most nights.

---

1. *Early mirrors which the men blamed for the dissatisfaction of their women.*

Chapter Fifteen

LM-2

"Scowling is like frowning but with more swear words."–James the Strong

Over the years, the Foreigners and their whole "let's take care of our planet" stance had begun to grate on those in the city.

Who cared about the state of wild hemp or the "stroke—don't eat—a four-legged creature" campaign? Most in the city just wanted the Foreigners to shut up and make things—like their statues. In fact, those from the city would have happily run the Foreigners into the outlands, if it wasn't for their statues and the discovery of the reflectors—a discovery stumbled onto by Loud Mouth's granddaughter; LM-2.

LM-2 was a quiet teenager with a brilliant brain who had been assigned to babysit Manifesto the Great, a boy who loved to collect things.

From the time he could walk, he rummaged, hoarded, and recreated and soon found his way to the Foreigner's Art Centre. Manifesto the Great found comfort there; it was so much more fun than loitering around the library and its smelly books.

There was a sense of fluidity about the place, a respect for life, although a child of ten wouldn't use such words. He could not resist returning again and again.

He liked the reading devices, the studios full of recycled materials,

and the way men and women worked together, taking turns shouting—
a place where women like the mother he loved seemed to lead a
happier life.

By the time he was ten, it was his place of refuge from a father who
scowled at him.

The Foreigners all embraced the next leader; they doted on him,
ruffled his hair, laughed at his funny ways—all apart from LM-2. The
last thing she wanted to do was babysit.

She took him on long walks, and Manifesto the Great collected to
his heart's content—plants, rocks, and shells, including the pearl
reflector shell.

"These would be great for adjusting one's own wig," he said to
LM-2.

She looked down at Manifesto the Great's eager eyes and was on
the verge of dismissing him when she caught sight of her distorted face
reflected in the inside of the shell . . .

She lifted it.

"A reflector," she said. "I see what you mean."

Manifesto the Great looked at her. "You could upcycle."

She laughed. "Bit more than upcycle—maybe reinvent."

He jumped. "Can I watch?"

The Foreigners laughed at LM-2's ideas of reflection, apart from
Manifesto the Great.

"Get back to your babysitting walks," they said.

LM-2 ignored them. She knew she had stumbled onto something,
and it wasn't long before she and Manifesto the Great had bonded over
the art of inventing.

Their first mirror was pocket-sized.

Manifesto the Great, desperate to impress his father, couldn't wait
to show him.

He slid the reflector into a box and presented it to his father across
the breakfast table.

James the Strong opened the box with Aggie and the Librarian watching.

Manifesto the Great talked of how "LM-2 designed it" and how he was "allowed to watch *and* help."

Aggie listened; a pang of jealousy stabbed her heart. "Who's this LM-2?" she snapped.

"Just a Foreigner," he muttered.

James the Strong stared at his reflection with disappointment.

"This is my face?" he muttered.

He turned to Aggie. "You called me handsome."

"You are," she said.

He looked again. Thank pickle for my magnificent family member, he thought.

"You get used to it," said the Librarian.

James the Strong continued to stare.

"Looking like everyone else," said the Librarian.

"Not sure I want to," muttered James the Strong.

"You'll be the first to have one," said his son.

He waited for praise.

"You could practice your speeches with it."

James the Strong turned to his son. "And what's wrong with my speeches?"

The reflectors weren't exactly a hit with the Foreigners either. Turned out no one liked what they saw, and they cursed LM-2 for her stupid discovery.

"Here we are running out of materials to make their ridiculous statues," snapped her father, a man nothing like Loud Mouth, "and what are you doing? Stripping the shores of shells and making stupid reflectors to remind us of how ugly we really are?"

LM-2 talked of a feeling in her bones that the reflectors would lead to something more. No one listened. Instead, she was ordered to accompany the rebels on their next "storming the meeting" mission, which LM-2 claimed was "a waste of time."

Every man in the city wanted a statue. Having a statue gave a man hero status, made women more malleable—being owned by a hero was better than being owned by a mere man—and soon led to the laying of flowers at the feet of statues. There were even competitions, which led to flower-stripping and another thing for the Foreigners to complain about.

The Foreigners could not recycle fast enough to keep up with the city's demands, and many saw a future of bleak landscapes and bugger-all plants.

"If they keep on with this flower-stripping, then what will the wasp-killers live off . . . and where will we be?" shouted LM-2's father. "Overrun, dying like flies from their stings. We need to storm the meetings," he said, "be heard."

No one else had a better idea, so the Foreigners regularly stormed the readers' meetings, demanding to be heard and having rights. Not much happened . . . they never made it past the door. The Librarian, with a "noted" sniff, shoed them away like flies, slamming the door in their faces.

LM's father turned to LM-2.

"You have spent time with the son," he said. "Perhaps you can influence the father?"

Me? thought LM-2. *What the frig can I do?* And she was about to say just that when she caught her father's steely glare.

He was on the verge of swearing, bursting into one of his rants about the excessive use of trees without replacing.

"There's more to you than reflections," he said. "You have a persuasive power about you . . . you just need to harness it." And before she could argue or ask him to explain, he left the room.

Chapter Sixteen

THE STORMING

"Four-legged creatures come in many sizes. Readers attempted to catalogue them, but making up names was not their strong point, until Earth was discovered."–the Librarian's diary

$\mathcal{T}$he two allocated rebel Foreigners disguised LM-2 as a man and pushed their way into the library. LM-2, having been trained to speak in a deep voice and butt into conversations, made a passing resemblance to a young teenage boy with way more growing to do.

On LM-2's suggestion, they watched and waited for the Librarian to leave. Manifesto the Great knew all about the Librarian's habits.

Foreigner One knocked on the door.

"Bet you they won't let us in," said Foreigner Two.

"You say that every time," said Foreigner One.

"Yes, well, there is a reason for that."

"We have a right to be heard," yelled Foreigner Two with a bang on the door.

"They'll just send for that snotty Librarian," said Foreigner One. "Complete waste of time."

LM-2 wondered. Manifesto the Great said the readers were idiots, nothing without the Librarian.

"I heard something," she lied. "At the door."

"Me too," lied Foreigner Two.

LM-2 hammered the door. "I know you're in there."

"Go away," hissed a voice from behind the door.

"We have something of interest," she said.

"Interest?" said Reader One.

"The reflectors," lied LM-2, "and I'm working on a bigger size . . ."

"Reflectors?" said Reader One. He creaked the door open to a crack; Foreigner One shoved his foot in.

"Don't mention that word near the boss," said Reader One.

"Boss?" said LM-2.

"James the Strong."

"We just call him the boss," said Reader One. "To keep his spirits up."

Reader Two appeared from behind with a "Shhhh—he hears through walls."

"We've arranged to meet with the Librarian," LM-2 lied as Foreigner One edged the door open.

"The Librarian is busy—seeing to the boss," hissed Reader One with a sideways glance. "He's not himself."

"The Librarian?" said Foreigner One.

"The boss," said Reader One.

"More a grumpy old man than a man's man," said Reader One.

Reader Two threw him a "too much information" look.

"Well, he is," snapped Reader One. "A right pain in the proverbial. Rarely laughs, let alone listens to a joke, and that new voice of his goes right through me like a dose of . . . constipation water."

The men pulled a face.

"Used to love listening to him, now it's like the screech of a hen mid shag," said Reader One.

The men chuckled.

"Shhhh," hissed LM-2. "Was that footsteps? Let us in."

The Foreigners pushed at the door.

The readers pushed back.

"Why don't we talk somewhere else?" said Reader Two. "Meetings aren't what they used to be."

The Foreigners looked at each other. "Somewhere else? Then it won't be a meeting, and you won't be bound to do anything."

"We'll write things down," said Reader One.

"Pfff, and then what?" muttered Foreigner Two.

"Look, just go away," said Reader Two, "and we'll talk of this later. He'll be here any minute."

The Foreigner didn't budge.

"Is it true? Does the, err . . . boss sleep alone?" said Foreigner Two, getting into the swing of things.

Reader One stopped. "How did you know?"

Reader Two nudged a "shut it."

"If only we had the old appointment system," muttered Reader One. "And a few willing females . . ." He stopped as James the Strong appeared from the shadows, looming over the Foreigners.

"There is no such thing as a willing female," he said.

The Foreigners jumped.

"A mere myth," stuttered Foreigner One with a nervous smile.

James the Strong eyed the Foreigner.

"Why are you here?"

"Democracy," snapped Foreigner Two.

Reader One almost chuckled.

James the Strong threw him a look and, with a small fart, pushed open the door. Foreigner Two, a brave man, marched in behind him, followed by LM-2 and Foreigner One.

James the Strong eased himself into a chair and slid his feet onto the table, and before the readers had time to usher the Foreigners out, Foreigner Two jumped in. "We're here to defend the planet, protect things . . ."

"Boss doesn't need to hear this," muttered Reader Two.

"We're running out of materials," said Foreigner Two.

"Just chop down more trees," said Reader Two.

"And when we run out of trees?" said Foreigner Two.

"Who cares," sighed James the Strong.

"The thing is, we can't replace a tree," said LM-2.

"As if," said the two readers in unison.

James the Strong eyed the teenager's *sweet* face . . .

"We told them to go away," said Reader One.

James the Strong sniffed. "How about we shut these windows? Can't move for the smell of flowers these days. It's bad enough having all these statues everywhere, but covered in flowers—that's air pollution, that is. Makes me feel quite heady."

"Quite, sir . . . err, boss," muttered Reader Two, quickly moving to a window.

James the Strong turned to the Foreigners. "Did you know there is not one of me?"

"One?" said Foreigner Two.

"Statue," said James the Strong. "There is not one statue of me. And even if there was, can't see Aggie leaving flowers, let alone that son of hers."

He looked at LM-2. "Are you that Loud Mouth's son?"

"Grandson."

"Grandson?" James eyed LM-2's feminine stance. "Heard of a granddaughter, not a son . . ."

"LM-2 here is but a mere student," said Foreigner Two.

"Still learning," said Foreigner One.

"That idiot grandfather of yours nearly had Wife-ie believing in stupid recycling," muttered James the Strong.

"Recycling is not exactly stupid," said Foreigner One.

"It keeps things tidy," said LM-2.

"My father was always tidying up," said James the Strong. "There wasn't a sock drawer in his room not color-coded, and quite frankly I found it boring."

"Yes, but we are not talking of drawers, we are talking of recycling and statues," said Foreigner Two.

"I hate recycling," muttered James the Strong.

"You can't hate recycling . . . it saves things," said Foreigner Two.

"Shall I just push them out, boss?" said Reader Two.

"And it's amazing what you can make with a few rubber bands and an old 'tastes like steak' packet," said LM-2. "Some would say artistic."

The readers gasped.

The word *artistic* enflamed James the Strong.

"Artistic? Artistic!"

James the Strong looked from one Foreigner to another; he stopped at LM-2. "You sure you're Loud Mouth's grandson?"

LM-2 nodded.

"You're as much like him as Manifesto . . ." James the Strong stopped, looked away, then pulled himself together. "Personally, I'd ban statues, but these bozos here reckon it could damage things."

"A bit of worship keeps the masses happy," said Reader One.

"What harm does it do?" said Reader Two.

"Well, breathing for a start," said James the Strong. "When the sun's up, the city smells like a good-old-fashioned nurturing shed on a busy day."

He chuckled at his wit.

"What about if we were to create something new?" said LM-2.

There was a sharp intake of breath. Manifesto the Great was not keen on anything "new" unless it was a shagging position.

LM-2 looked around. "Artistic?"

All glared at LM-2.

"Innovative?" jumped in Foreigner One.

James the Strong looked confused.

"You could go down in history," said LM-2.

"Hmm, history—I like that," muttered James the Strong.

He stopped. "History? For what?"

LM-2, lost for words, began to stutter about spaceships and recycling until James the Strong, confused, put up his hand.

"No one touches my spaceships."

"Now shall I push 'em out?" said Reader One with a smug look.

"Sir," said Foreigner One, "the touching of spaceships is merely for the benefit of your 'Arrival Day' celebrations."

"Oh," said James the Strong.

"Why yes, we like to keep things as authentic as possible for . . . err . . . .your pulling."

"Tell me more," said James the Strong.

Foreigner One, with more technical talk than an engineer, jumped in, using gestures and reenactments that had James the Strong listening with his "I understand look"—until the Librarian appeared and, with his usual damper on things, put an end to the meeting.

Chapter Seventeen

MIRRORS

"Large is a mere five-letter word."–LM-2

The Foreigners headed out of the city with no idea what to do next.

Foreigner One eyed LM-2. She had nearly landed them in it . . .

"What the hell was all that innovation stuff about?" said Foreigner Two.

"I was thinking on my feet," she said.

"Thinking on your feet? If it weren't for Himself talking about the spaceships, we'd have been strung up on a wall like those god-awful skins."

"I don't think so," she muttered.

"If you don't come up with something *innovative,* we'll be excommunicated—sent to the Aliens."

"Hardly," said LM-2. "We Foreigners do all the work—the city would shut down without us."

"She has a point," said Foreigner Two.

"And I have an idea," said LM-2.

"Pfff—you? An idea?" said Foreigner One.

"I was thinking about miniatures and reflectors and a way to use fewer materials for even bigger-looking statues."

The two men looked at her and for the first time saw a bit of Loud Mouth, except with way better hair.

"We could try reflecting something onto something else . . . bigger," she said.

The two male Foreigners were speechless. They had never heard of a woman making sense before, let alone a teenager.

LM-2 came up with the template involving mirrors and a miniature statue of James the Strong.

She, along with Manifesto the Great and the two Foreigners, had worked hard on the project, keeping it quiet from everyone until Manifesto the Great blurted it out across his morning toast.

James the Strong choked on his tea; the idea of a miniature was as offensive to him as being owned was to Aggie.

"Miniature? There is nothing miniature about me," shouted James the Strong.

"And there's mirrors as well," said Manifesto the Great.

"I'm scrapping the project," said James the Strong.

"But Dad."

Aggie nodded.

"Assign that teenager to babysitting."

Aggie stopped.

Ever since her son fell under the *spell* of LM-2, Aggie had a feeling in her bones, a shifting of things not in her favor.

Aggie knew *he* was a *she* straightaway. LM-2's "bum fluff" was as convincing as the sock stuffed down her trousers, and as for phallic jokes, they were as funny as the Librarian's, and he had no sense of humor. He didn't even flinch at a fart, which had most men in hysterics.

Aggie had tried to take charge, make some distance between her son and that so-called teenage boy, but there was a bond between them. LM-2 was all her son talked of, and everything Aggie did made things worse.

She stared at her son. Did she really want him spending even more time with *her*?

"Let's not be too hasty," she said.

"I thought babysitting was all the rage," said James the Strong.

Manifesto the Great looked from one parent to the other.

"Yes, but what if this miniature was more than, well, a miniature? It could be a coup," said Aggie.

"Coup?" said James the Strong.

"It's possible, Dad. Don't forget, there's mirrors too."

"You could go down in history," said Aggie.

"That's what that teenager said," muttered James the Strong.

Aggie huffed.

"What about a show then?" said Manifesto the Great.

James the Strong looked at Aggie, confused.

"Just us and the . . . Foreigners?"

James the Strong said nothing.

"And the mirrors," said Manifesto the Great.

The Foreigners, describing their new take on an old statue idea as "jaw dropping," arranged a demonstration by the waterfall at sunset.

"You will never look at a statue again in the same way," said LM-2.

James the Strong, suppressing weird feelings he now felt for this teenager, nodded.

Aggie, her son, the Librarian, and James the Strong stood by the waterfall as LM-2 (in man garb) slid a pocket-sized object covered in a hemp handkerchief onto a rock by the waterfall.

The two Foreigners waited, poised for light-switching.

James the Strong and his entourage stared in silence.

"Is this a joke?" snapped the Librarian.

LM-2 had worked tirelessly with the reflectors, up all night, convincing herself it would work. Now, in the sharp light of the sunset, she wondered. She tugged at the hemp handkerchief; it fluttered from the figure. The group stared at the doll-like statue.

LM-2 gulped.

"Are you taking the piss?" said the Librarian.

"Just wait," muttered LM-2.

"My family member's larger than that," shouted James the Strong.

"A baby's family member's larger than that," said the Librarian with a look of distaste.

LM-2 nodded to her comrades.

Foreigner Two positioned the reflector to catch the sunset, and it reflected the light onto the miniature statue. James the Strong's majestic silhouette flashed behind the waterfall, filling the backdrop larger than a spaceship.

The effect was breathtaking.

"Immortalization," muttered James the Strong.

"Unbelievable," muttered the Librarian.

Manifesto the Great, jumping with joy, grabbed LM-2's hand.

Aggie's heart sank.

The Foreigners basked in their glory, slapping each other on the back.

Manifesto the Great turned to his father and waited for a smile, a nod, a "well done," and was just on the brink of shouting a "See, Dad?" when a cloud slid by, plunging the waterfall into darkness.

The cheering hushed.

The back-slapping stopped.

The cloud moved on. The sunset appeared, lighting up the waterfall . . .

They waited for the silhouette to appear. The light flickered, finally flashing the image of a Victorian Earth bedroom.

They stared into the cluttered room with no idea what a potted plant was.

"What the pickle?" muttered James the Strong.

An aging face appeared, her hair piled high, her face covered in makeup.

"Is that a woman?" muttered someone.

She began to apply more makeup.

"What's she doing?" muttered Manifesto the Great.

They shook their heads as a boy in a nightdress appeared from behind her.

"Mirror, mirror, on the wall." He laughed, bursting into tears as she clipped him over the ear.

Chapter Eighteen

EARTH

"No one realized they had aged until they saw their reflections.
They just thought it happened to other people."—The Librarian's
diary.

*J*ames the Strong's magnificent silhouette was overlooked
by the discovery of Earth, and yet again he sulked.

Soon, reflectors (now called "mirrors") were all the
rage, and any Settler worth a jot owned not only a mirror but several—
large and positioned to catch the sunset at every angle going. And once
a language adapter was developed, a whole new world opened up to the
planet.

Within a year, the Settlers were peering into the mirrors, reflecting
parts of lives Victorians called private. They stared into living rooms,
bedrooms, restaurants, and conference halls, quickly picking up the
difference between a bribe and a tip, interfering and advising, and a
fumble with staff and conjugal rights with "one's wife."

Anywhere there was a mirror, those in the city watched like a soap
opera.

The Incomers couldn't afford large mirrors. What they had were
pocket mirrors, which they took about their person, waiting for the
sunset—which, when arrived, sent them into a spin of "headless
chicken" running, trying to catch the light like an elusive mobile signal.

It took six months to develop an arial that connected to Earth and
another month for the production to be rolled out, leading to rows of

identical Incomer's huts covered in aerials and Incomers finishing a day's work "on the dot" to "catch the sunset."

The Foreigners were busier than ever, caught up making mirrors—with instructions—flat-pack aerials—with instructions—and price-cut Victorian clothes that were machine washable while trying to deal with an influx of old wigs to recycle.

Settler men had given up wigs for hats and beards and the amusing tipping of a hat in the street, along with "suffragette" joking, while women flounced about in dresses with petticoats, privately wondering if petticoat-wearing was really the be-all and end-all so many claimed.

The Settlers and the Incomers found the Victorians hugely funny. They laughed at the old-fashioned ideas of Darwinism and even had Darwinism parties, making up names for four-legged creatures, then falling about the floor laughing.

They learnt that owning a woman was called *marriage* and wedding dresses were best left for Darwinism parties due to white being the sort of color that could only be worn once before "needing a wash."

It was Fanny who first saw a suffragette.

She, being the offspring of the spokeswoman, was, as many called her, a chip off the old block and just as mouthy.

Fanny was staring into a tank-sized mirror wondering how long it would be before her owner would arrive looking for a "seeing to."

Her owner's idea of a "seeing to" was a quick in-and-out under a petticoat. An orgasm was a distant memory to Fanny, her family member comatose.

"It hasn't woken up in years," she often claimed, "let alone applauded an entry."

She stared at her image and was just in the middle of counting how many of her friends felt the same way when her image morphed into the bedroom of a suffragette.

She watched, fascinated, and over the next few months, a new world opened to her.

She started tea parties for women and talked of voting.

"It's the cornerstone of democracy," said Fanny over a particularly stewed cup of hemp tea.

"I thought democracy was standing outside the meeting room

yelling," said the aging horselike woman, "something the Foreigners did."

"Apparently not," said Fanny in her best "women from the mirror" accent.

The horselike woman sat up. With an accent like that, Fanny obviously knew what she was talking of.

LM-2 and her two comrades were installed in a room next to the meeting room. They were whipping up designs of mirrors that didn't rely on the sunsets, with switches and light adjustments.

Mirrors had changed everything, and Aggie struggled to adjust.

In a flash, LM-2 was in *her* library, and James the Strong was quoting *her* like she had the answer to everything . . . claiming LM-2 was the son he'd always dreamed of.

Gone was the man who depended on her. Instead, James the Strong was quoting a woman dressed as man who had her son eating out of her hand, and she, the mother of the next leader, had as much influence as an Alien.

She was as redundant as a used tea bag.

Aggie knew it was only a matter of time before James the Strong would work out exactly what the bulge in LM-2's groin really was. In fact, she often wondered if he already had.

She began to wake up in the morning in panic, look to the future with dread; soon her position would be as buggered as the flowered beds that were constantly stripped.

She thought and pondered and came to the conclusion that there was only one thing she could do to save herself: outthink LM-2 and interfere.

Before anyone could sneeze "statue," Aggie had come up with a template for a mirror that worked any time of the day.

The Foreigners, however, pooh-poohed her ideas; they had been told by the Librarian that she was a spy, not to be trusted.

Not that anyone trusted the Librarian, but at least he had some clout, could change things.

Aggie had as much clout as tea bag.

It was tough for LM-2, remaining incognito in a man's outfit. James the Strong loved to stand beside her and inhale her scent while she explained things so clearly, like Aggie used to.

LM-2 tried to keep her distance, but he was so large and the room so small, and he was always touching . . .

"You make everything so clear-cut—like sliced cheese," James the Strong said to her, literally breathing down her neck.

The truth was, she was starting to enjoy it. For a start, he had very pleasant-smelling armpits, and he always came to her—rather than the other two Foreigners—with a "let's hear what our LM-2 has to say."

"Merely tactile," muttered Foreigner One, who had taken to talking like the Librarian, "a habit to hide any confusion. This whole mirror thing has him flummoxed."

"As confused as a four-legged creatures after a day in a hemp field," muttered Foreigner Two.

"I wouldn't let him hear you say that," muttered LM-2.

"Doubt he'd understand," said Foreigner Two.

"He just needs gentle guidance," muttered LM-2 to herself. "A little time, that's all."

"Yes," muttered Foreigner One, "he is but a flummoxed creature."

Foreigner Two looked at his comrade. "Just cause you're best buddies with that Librarian doesn't mean you have to talk like him."

"Best buddies?" said Foreigner One.

"Yeah, you're so far up his backside you could clean his teeth."

"That is a highly inappropriate comment," said Foreigner One.

"Oh, I forgot, he's got falsies, hasn't he," snapped Foreigner Two.

"Falsies are for Incomers. What he has is a set of . . ." He turned to LM-2. "What do you call 'em?"

"New teeth," she sighed.

"New teeth for an old face," said Foreigner Two.

"You're so flippant," huffed Foreigner One.

"Oh am I? I'm not the one flicking his golden locks at a man old enough to be his grandfather."

Foreigner One glared at his comrade. "I am merely trying to oil the works for us," he hissed. "He is the only one who can make changes."

"Oil? You're so slippery you've got skid marks," snapped Foreigner Two, "on your tongue."

"It doesn't matter what age the Librarian is. We need to focus on these mirrors—work together—or we'll be back to the arts corner, achieving nothing," said LM-2.

"Yeah, like you want to go back," said Foreigner Two.

"Leave it," said Foreigner One.

LM-2 stopped. "What are you on about?"

"We've seen the way you look when *he* comes in," said Foreigner Two. "You'd better be careful."

"What do you mean?"

"I said leave it," snapped Foreigner One.

"I wouldn't get any ideas. That Aggie's still got her feet under a few tables."

"That's enough," snapped Foreigner One, gesturing to the corridor full of voices.

"That *Aggie* will be here any minute, and we need to be prepared. You know what that Librarian thinks of her."

Chapter Nineteen

THE RIFT

"Emotions ran deep in the Librarian, despite his pinched face."– Aggie

*A*ggie had already left a template with the Foreigners, and they had no idea what to do.

They were in the hub of the city helping to make decisions. One whiff of "Aggie loyalty" could screw it all up, cheese the Librarian right off.

"What shall we do?" hissed Foreigner One. "Lie? Pretend a four-legged creature has eaten them?"

The Librarian was in the meeting room listening. He spent hours spying, nearly as many as watching earthlings.

He watched the arresting of Emmeline Pankhurst, gasped at Sweeney Todd, laughed at Harold Lloyd, and shed a tear for Charlie Chaplin's Tramp.

The earthlings fascinated him. He loved intrigue, spying, and melo-drama as much as he loved *his* library, and if he could get all three at once, he was a man in heaven.

He tried to educate his esteemed leader of such things, but James the Strong preferred watching trams.

Planet Hy Man had sleek transporters that zipped about the street. All the Incomers had one, and all the Settlers had a driver along with one (usually an Incomer who didn't talk too much). No one used four-legged creatures to pull things, which confused James the Strong, and a confused James the Strong turned to women.

Which had the Librarian wondering . . .

He knew there was something funny about that LM-2. Why did she wear a cap inside?

A smile spread across his thin lips. He saw an opening . . .

Maybe his luck had turned.

He slid into the Foreigners' room and left minutes later . . . just as Aggie's heels echoed down the empty corridor.

Foreigner Two, with a flustered rummage, pulled out Aggie's template.

"It's going to be brutal," he said.

The footsteps stopped at the door.

"Brutal?" said Foreigner One. "You?"

"You heard what the Librarian said."

Aggie tapped a knock on the door.

"Aggie's no spy," said LM-2.

"Just follow my lead," hissed Foreigner Two.

Aggie knocked again.

"Your lead? I think you'll find it's my lead," snapped Foreigner One.

"She may be a know-it-all pain in the butt, but she's no spy," said LM-2. "I should know."

The two Foreigners stopped.

"Babysitting her son hardly gives you inside information," snapped Foreigner Two. He turned to his comrade. "Let me do the talking, you're too sensitive."

Foreigner One shrugged as Foreigner Two nodded at LM-2 to open the door.

"I wouldn't trust that Librarian as far as I can sneeze," she mumbled. "Spy my foot."

"Just open the door," hissed Foreigner Two as Aggie burst in.

"I was thinking about that last idea."

No one looked at her.

Aggie cleared the table of mugs and unrolled her latest template.

"I think I have a way of bypassing the sunset," she said.

The Foreigners looked at each other. Foreigner Two, with a sniff of indifference, unrolled another template. "We have our own ideas."

Aggie stared at it.

"That's my template."

"Hardly," said the Foreigner Two.

"It's in *my* handwriting," said Aggie.

"Could be mine," muttered Foreigner Two.

"Or mine," said Foreigner One.

Foreigner Two threw him a "leave it to me" glare.

Aggie eyed LM-2.

"Or perhaps yours?"

LM-2 glanced at Foreigner Two.

"Hardly," he said. "*She* would not have done that—or *that*." He thrust a pointed finger at the template.

"It's hardly groundbreaking," muttered Foreigner One, ignoring his comrade's "leave it" glare.

Aggie fumed. Her face hot, she made to argue but stopped as Foreigner Two pushed the template back to Aggie.

"We don't need this."

"Yeah," said Foreigner One.

Aggie fumbled with her template. Perhaps marching into the room wasn't the best thing . . .

The Librarian, listening in the next room, rubbed his hands with glee, and when he heard Aggie leave with a slam, he headed to his esteemed leader. He had a few more seeds to plant . . .

❖

James the Strong had no idea what was going on; all this *Earth stuff* had his brain buzzing like a bumblebee in a jar.

He stared at the waterfall from the window in his "man cave" and sighed. He was tired of stomping and looking like he understood.

He had spent hours in front of the mirror and his head was bursting with all the effort, and he still couldn't see what all the fuss was about.

Thank God for that wonderful LM-2, he thought. *My only port in the storm.*

"We are watching progress in the making," said the Librarian, marching in with two hemp teas.

He handed a mug to James the Strong, caught a glimpse of his "acting like he understood" look, and regretted his statement.

The concept of progress made as much sense to James the Strong as marriage—which, as he pointed out, was just a stupid way of spelling "owning."

"There is the ceremony," said the Librarian, "and rings."

"Pfff, that ol' chestnut," said James the Strong, who had no idea what the Librarian was talking about.

He looked out the window again as the Librarian began to adjust James the Strong's mirror.

"Why use four-legged creatures for pulling?"

The Librarian stopped. "What?"

"I can pull a spaceship quicker than those wheeled thingies," he muttered. "Why are we watching such idiots?"

The Librarian grunted.

"I'm fed up with these mirrors."

"I was thinking we try another position," muttered the Librarian.

James the Strong started. "Position?"

"The mirror," said the Librarian.

"Oh, I see—yes of course," muttered James the Strong.

The Librarian, with a quizzical look at his leader, continued.

"I was thinking if we move these mirrors about, we may find something different for you to view."

James the Strong nodded.

"Perhaps something more appealing?"

"Appealing?" said James the Strong. "I like that idea."

"Have you heard of the melodrama?" said the Librarian, moving into action.

James the Strong said nothing. The Librarian had gone for the largest mirror in the room with his pinwheel arms.

"Bit heavier than I thought," puffed the Librarian.

"You did pick the biggest mirror," said James the Strong.

The Librarian grunted. "Just thinking about the view, sir." He wobbled, attempted a step, failed, and, with a muffled "going down," toppled to the floor.

Manifesto watched as the mirror settled on top of his colleague, covering all but a well-polished sole of a high-heeled shoe.

He stared at the foot.

"Suppose you want me to help?" said James the Strong.

"Perhaps if you could, Your Graciousness," groaned the Librarian.

James the Strong eased the mirror up like it was an earring and waited for the Librarian to adjust himself.

"Would you like me to put it back?" said James the Strong.

"No, no," said the Librarian, dusting himself off. "Now that it's down . . . we must but continue."

He paused, looking around the room.

James the Strong waited.

Silence . . .

"You sure you don't want me to put it back?" said James the Strong, waving the mirror about like it was a hanky.

The Librarian, lost in thought, gestured an "I'm thinking."

James the Strong tutted.

"Hmmm, now, yes . . ." muttered the Librarian.

"It will soon be sunset," huffed James the Strong. "I could have this back in a jiff-like."

"If we move that to there and this here," said the Librarian.

"Right," said James the Strong.

"No, wait, maybe there . . ." said the Librarian.

"OK," muttered James the Strong.

"No, I think here, or over there?" said the Librarian. "Yes, that's it. Now let's just tweak this mirror."

"Tweet?" James the Strong looked confused. "In my man cave?"

"It is *tweak*, sir—*tweet* is something birds do."

James the Strong, pretending he didn't hear, snapped a "Hurry up . . ."

"Yes, nearly there. Just need to move the four-legged skins."

James the Strong glared at him.

Aggie walked down the corridor, her template crumbled by LM-2's feet, forgotten. Never had she felt so vulnerable and alone.

Chapter Twenty

MELODRAMA

"Mornings were a thing of beauty until the bathroom mirror was invented."—James the Strong

*T*wo hours later, James the Strong's mood was at the teeth-clenching stage as the Librarian tweaked at a level that had him sweating like a wrestler in a heat wave.

His bed was now covered in shoes and cushions with his breakable-as-an-eggshell, hand-painted-with-love skull lamp precariously balanced on top. And on the floor, piled in a heap like garbage bags, having been ripped from the walls like used waxing strips, was his much-loved, took-forever-to-collect, four-legged-creature skin collections.

He stared down at his tea, now colder than Aggie's "not tonight" look, and wondered just who was the boss.

"We're nearly there," muttered the Librarian with smugness.

James the Strong wanted to slap him.

"Nearly there? Look what you have done to my room. I may as well lock the door and run away."

The Librarian, with a dismissive wave, muttered an "easily fixed," then pulled out his mock Victorian fob watch. "It's sunset—any moment now, sir."

James the Strong plonked himself onto the pile of four-legged creatures' skins as the Librarian handed him his iced tea.

A Victorian stage appeared on the mirror. Applause rippled from it, and a smart young gentleman sauntered onto the stage followed by a woman with blood red lips, messy hair, and runny eyeliner. Within minutes, James the Strong was engrossed as the "gentleman" talked to the woman like she had a pea for a brain.

He was on the edge of his seat.

The gentleman was so masterful, so commanding. *If only I could be like him,* thought James the Strong, *Aggie would be back in my bed like there was no tomorrow, maybe even wearing some complicated Victorian underwear . . .*

He sighed. So much fun to undress.

"Get out of my house, you damnable harlot," shouted the gentleman.

Aggie, who usually skidded past the man cave as quickly as possible, stopped. *Harlot?*

She peered in, caught sight of the Librarian beside the leader perched on a pile of skins, and stopped.

They looked up, James the Strong with a look she had only seen after a particularly rousing applause from a speech.

"Did you just call me a harlot?" she said.

"Ma'am, it is but the mirror." The Librarian smiled unconvincingly.

Aggie ventured into the man cave, eyeing the pile of four-legged creatures' skins with a confused "what the pickle" look.

"Now that is what I call a man," muttered James the Strong.

Aggie stared at the mirror.

"And you can take your damnable orphans with you," shouted the gentleman.

Applause filled the room, along with cheering.

"You tell her, gov," shouted someone from the audience.

"I think that's a play—a melodrama," said Aggie.

"You damnable woman, what would you know?" said James the Strong.

Aggie, with a pinched face, glared.

"Shall I cover the mirror for a while?" said the Librarian with no intention of doing so.

James the Strong rose from his pile of skins; Aggie's reaction had spurred him on. He'd shut her up with one command.

"Now get out!" he yelled, then faltered. "Take in some morning air."

"Morning air? It's sunset," she said.

"It won't be for long, you harlot," snapped James the Strong.

"Sir," said the Librarian. "Harlots are not spoken of here."

"I'll do what I damn well please," snapped James the Strong. "Now toddle off, you trophy of mine."

"Well, really," flustered Aggie.

"Yes, really," said James the Strong.

The Librarian threw a twisted smile at Aggie.

"And clean your wedding dress," said James the Strong.

Aggie stood dumbstruck. "I have no wedding dress," she muttered.

"Sir," muttered the Librarian. "Perhaps we could do a spot of head-clearing—outside?"

"Head? My head is as clear as that water running from that . . . that, err . . ." He gestured to the window.

"Waterfall?" said Aggie.

The Librarian, with yet another slappable smug look, said nothing.

He had no idea it would be so easy.

If one play had this effect, what would the silent movies do to his leader?

"Sir, there is no need for you to carry on like this." He feigned another smile. "Aggie is, after all, *your* woman."

"Carry on!" said James the Strong. "The leader never carries on." And with a dramatic point to the door, he shouted, "Now get out, woman, and let me see the end of this damnable melodrama."

Within a week, James the Strong was addicted to melodramas and had taken to pacing up and down the corridor, talking like he was in one.

He couldn't believe how yelling changed things, how good it felt—way better than being confused and pretending. Aggie stopped being such a smart-arse, and the readers stood to attention when he marched in, although they did talk of toning things down, which James the Strong chose to ignore.

Toning things down made as much sense as the Earth's snail's-pace tram system. Angry worked. All he had to do was look angry . . . scowl and men scattered, except of course when he spoke to that rather nice young teenager. The last thing he wanted to do was yell at that sweet face.

The Librarians watched and smiled. Soon, that damnable Aggie and her liberal advice would be gone for good, and then he could manipulate. He felt smug, pleased with himself, until the Readers called an extra meeting and talked of "prepping."

In those days, prepping was the nearest thing to a coup and only ever done in a state of emergency. In fact, there had only ever been one: when the four-legged creatures rampaged the main street during Arthur of the North's reign.

Troops of Aliens appeared from nowhere, surprising the creatures, and, with the sort of herding any shepherd would be proud of, cleared the streets.

The readers wondered if James the Strong could be herded back to his sulking room, preferably with the door locked.

"We need to do something," said Reader One. "The last thing we need is other men copying him, shouting 'damnable' at their women."

He looked at his colleague. He had heard of Fanny's suffragette tea parties and her talk of such things as *voting*—whatever that was.

"Some of those women are getting lippy," he said. "Imagine if they got wind of this slapping! There could be an uprising, like the Aliens and the four-legged creatures all those years ago."

"Uprising?" shouted James the Strong as he entered the meeting room. "Who is uprising and why wasn't I told before now?"

"There is no uprising, boss," said Reader Two.

"But we do need to set up a system," muttered Reader Two, who, in a panic, waffled on about leakage and damage control, which had even him confused.

James the Strong held up his hand, silencing the reader, as the Librarian entered with his best "I know what to do" expression. He was about to say something profound when Aggie's heels clipped down the corridor . . .

She was heading for LM-2's room.

She had more than a template to retrieve—she had her dignity.

"It's that Aggie causing all this uprising, isn't it?" boomed James the Strong.

Aggie stopped . . .

"That damnable woman." James the Strong looked at the Librarian. "Has she been stirring things up?"

"You did call her a harlot," muttered Reader One.

"Yes, but harlots are known for their underwear, and I was hoping . . ." James the Strong stopped, realizing the meeting room was not the place to bring up underwear.

The Foreigners, hearing the shouting, appeared from their rooms. They caught sight of Aggie poised in the corridor.

"Perhaps, sir, you've rubbed her up the wrong way—again," muttered Reader Two.

James the Strong looked around the room. *They are so smug.*

"Rubbing her up the wrong way? *Hell and damnation*, that woman could do with some wrong rubbing. In fact, *rubbing is too good for her*," shouted James the Strong.

The Foreigners looked at Aggie with a "glad it's you and not me" look.

Aggie blushed . . .

"What she needs is a good slap," shouted James the Strong.

The readers, the Foreigners, even the Librarian gasped.

Slap?

Slapping was something Foreigners did with rugs, to get the dust out.

Am I but a mere rug?

Aggie looked from the two Foreigners to LM-2, her face now poker red.

"I heard that!" she shouted.

Oh, bugger, thought James the Strong. *Did I go too far . . . ?*

The Librarian, thinking on his feet, grabbed his chance.

"Rather than slap," he said to James the Strong, "perhaps it's time for a change of things . . . woman-wise? Remove any opposition?"

For a week, Aggie flounced as she had never flounced before, but it did her little good.

The Librarian saw to that.

With the hearing of a sheepdog, the nose of a sniffer dog, and the ability to pick up conversation better than any bugging equipment, he mingled like mad. From the top of society to the bottom, from the rich to the minions, he spread "slapping" gossip about Aggie.

He could lip-read like the deaf, camouflage like a chameleon, and move among a crowd as unnoticed as a beggar, which he often did, spreading rumors, gossips, and leaflets claiming that Aggie was known to "slap the leader."

He even ventured to the outposts where the Aliens and the Foreigners traded.

"Should our esteemed leader live with a slapper?" he said, along with the many leaflets he circulated.

Aggie was outcast, banished, and with just a small bag and her "if all else fails" plan, she left.

In one week, she had gone from a woman who could wander and boss to a woman no one spoke to, pushed out like a sack of used hemp.

Chapter Twenty-One

A SLAP IN THE FACE

"A closed door can always open again."–Fanny

*T*he city was dark and quiet except for the odd scurry of a rat. Aggie, with her small bag, stared into the empty street thinking how shit her "if all else fails" plan was.

It started and ended with a tent.

She hadn't factored in the need for pitching . . .

She had heard of Fanny's "suffragette teas" held in a house so big it would take all morning to jog around the gardens.

Perhaps there was a small square in the garden for her tent? A corner, until she knew what to do?

Fanny opened the door with a startled look. She had heard the rumors . . .

"Who's that?" shouted a male voice.

"Oh, no one," Fanny said with a "go away" look.

"If it's that slapper, you know what to do," he shouted.

"I didn't slap," muttered Aggie.

She looked at Fanny's "not here" face and realized pitching a tent in her garden was as probable as the Librarian telling the truth.

Fanny slid a card into her hand.

"You're not alone," she whispered.

"I see," muttered Aggie.

"Try the women's quarters," she whispered and slammed the door shut with a "she's gone."

Aggie, confused, looked at the card.

"The underground is strong!"

The women's quarters were a good hour's walk. Aggie headed off in the dark with hopes of womanly understanding—despite the fact that she had never been there.

She knocked on the Warden's door.

The Warden slid open the peephole and eyed Aggie with a pinched smile.

"Who's that?" shouted a distant male voice.

"Oh, nothing." The Warden nervously laughed, poking a card at her. "Try the Foreigners," she whispered.

A man appeared behind the woman and looked at Aggie like she had the plague.

Aggie eyed the gruff face.

"Slappers aren't welcome here," he said.

And before Aggie could say "I didn't slap," the peephole slid shut.

"No need to be so mean," said the woman from behind the door as Aggie, confused, disheartened, and heading toward fearful, stared at the card.

"The underground will win!"

She headed for the arts corner. It, too, was an hour's walk in the dark with little light.

She stood at the gate and rang the bell, setting off a searchlight and a litter of four-legged creatures barking. Two bleary-eyed male Foreigners appeared from nowhere.

"You can take your slapping and bugger off," muttered one.

He turned off the lights while the other ushered the four-legged creatures away.

"But I don't slap," she muttered into the dark.

No one answered, but a leaflet fluttered from the gate.

"The underground will never die!"

This time with a date and an address.

Aggie slid it into her pocket along with the others and decided to leave the city.

PART TWO

A true leader masks his feelings.
A smart leader knows what is needed and how to convince the masses it's what they demand.
Manifesto the Great, like Arthur of the North, was a master of all three.

Chapter Twenty-Two

THE FUNERAL

"The only good Foreigner is a sleeping one."–the Librarian

Earth time: 1920s

*M*anifesto the Great was not always *great*, but he had from the age of ten always been *small*, with little hair, tiny feet, and—some say—little other things.

It was he who had started the whole "short is the new tall" idea after realizing that his father had lied to him.

Manifesto the Great had been an artistic boy with a passion for cheering his mother up. But when he was told she had been eaten by a four-legged creature, he had nightmares for weeks, vowing to rid the city of "every four-legged creature standing."

He was forty-five when his eighty-year-old father died, just like Arthur of the North—stung by a wasp—and just like Arthur of the North, he passed away in a blur of visions . . .

In the forty-five years since James the Strong had taken charge, the city had evolved into a metropolis: penthouses for the Settlers with views and clean air and low living areas for the Incomers with the smells of effluent, air fresheners, and taxis that honked like their lives depended on it.

It was a noisy, masculine place full of beating drums and orders chanted like a Muslim's call to prayer.

Manifesto the Great grasped his leadership with a speech prepared since the loss of his mother. As the drums beat out the coming of a new leader, he marched onto the speech balcony, stood on a box, and inhaled the smell of power.

The Librarian, now in a wheelchair, wheeled himself beside his prodigy. He peered over the balcony and stared down at the minions of men, along with the odd woman free of a child.

"Great pickling egg, there's some crowd today," he coughed.

Manifesto the Great said nothing. A crowd to the Librarian was anything more than two people in a canteen queue.

LM-2 was by her lover's body on the burial bed (a misleading name, as the dead were burnt on Planet Hy Man). She could hear Manifesto the Great begin his speech, but she wasn't listening.

Her heart ached, emotions and memories bubbling inside her. She had spent her life making sense of James the Strong's confusion.

Now she had her freedom.

She looked at her lover's smooth face; there was not a wrinkle. He had died before his time.

If only, she thought and blew her nose, unsettling the mechanical bird perched on the windowsill.

"My father wanted the best for everyone," shouted Manifesto the Great. "He was a person for the people."

The footman bent near the leader's ear.

"There no need to shout," he said, "the voice-vibrator is on."

Manifesto the Great looked impressed.

"Yes—your voice will echo across the courtyard to the outskirts of the city."

"Even the women at home?" said Manifesto the Great.

"Who cares about the women?" muttered the Librarian.

"If the women have their windows open," muttered the footman.

Manifesto the Great waved to the crowd. "And the Aliens?"
The Librarian belched.

"Let's not get carried away, sir," muttered the footman.

The footmen were the initiation of Manifesto the Great.

The Foreigners were arming themselves with knowledge, secretly educating their young. Manifesto the Great saw them as a threat and came up with idea of divide-and-suppression using privileges.

The number of readers had swelled since Aggie left, and they met in a large room at the top of the library. It had the best view, but there was a fair walk to the beverage department.

"Imagine," said Manifesto the Great to his father once, "if you had footmen . . ."

"Footmen?" said James the Strong, confused.

"Bit like a servant," said the Librarian, "but better dressed."

"They could run up and down with drinks," said Manifesto the Great, "giving your readers more time to think."

"It *is* a long walk to the beverage machine," muttered his father . . .

James the Strong soon loved the idea and, inspired by Queen Victoria's footmen, suggested a uniform as out of place in the city as crochet bikini.

Soon, anyone who was anyone had a footman, and a "do" was not a "do" without a footman standing to attention in the background. A footman gave a sense of affluence and power, especially when barked at with orders.

The Foreigners' united front cracked as they lost many good men to the promise of luxury and the odd frustrated rich woman looking for a bit of bed-diving. In fact, it was the ambition of many young Foreigners'—way better than the production line of a factory.

Manifesto the Great looked down at his speech. Then, imitating his father's purring voice, he began his tribute to his father.

"My father grasped innovation with both hands . . ."

LM-2 could hear the crowd rumble.

She closed his eyes and placed a hemp-covered button on each, then walked out onto the speech balcony.

The Librarian tried to intercept her with a curt wheelie at her heels. She sidestepped him like she had done a million times before.

She tugged at Manifesto the Great, who was waving to a cheering crowd.

"I am going now," she shouted, "to the outlands."

"What did you say?" said Manifesto the Great mid wave.

"She said she's going to the outlands," shouted the Librarian, sparking a coughing fit.

The footman handed the Librarian a tissue.

"I said I'm leaving . . ." She stopped. In the distance was a cloaked woman with a familiar walk.

The Librarian, still coughing, began to choke.

Manifesto the Great slapped the Librarian on the back.

The Librarian pushed him away.

"Keep waving, boy . . ." He stopped, catching sight of the cloaked figure astride a giant turtle.

The noise of the crowd faded as a woman in the cloak of an Alien weaved her way through the men.

Manifesto the Great stared.

Her stance was familiar.

"Shit," said the Librarian.

"Mother?" said Manifesto the Great.

Chapter Twenty-Three

THE TENT

"There had to be a better place to live for a woman than a place where you could lose everything just because the father of your child called you harlot."—Aggie

Forty-five years ago

*A*ggie woke up with a dry throat. She peered at the inside of her tent and stretched . . .

I'm definitely doing the right thing, she told herself despite the sore neck, back, and hip *and* the ant crawling across her forehead. She brushed it off, sweating under the hot, limp canvas.

She, like all from the city, had heard myths of the outlands[1] and told herself she wanted to find out the real story.

The truth was, she had nowhere else to go.

She had tried to find a place to stay, knocking on many doors, but all she got were cryptic comments and doors slammed in her face.

She stared at the sun beaming in through the tent and began to sweat. She had her template and three dubious cards. *A big help when you're looking for a safe place to raise your son . . .*

She heard a rustle of grass, an "away with you now," a series of warm animal grunts, and a "what's this I wonder, Dixie?"

Aggie peered through the opening of the tent and straight into the soft brown eyes of a large four-legged creature. It peered back, its lips moist from hemp-munching.

Aggie rubbed her eyes; she had never seen a four-legged creature before, let alone got a whiff of its' breath.

"Come away with you, Dixie," said a soft female voice.

Aggie looked up and stared into the brown face of an Alien.

The Alien looked at Aggie as she rubbed the top of Dixie's head.

"You can't camp here," she said. "This is a soya field—you'll flatten it before it's ready."

"I didn't know," stuttered Aggie.

The Alien peered inside the tent. There wasn't much there, just a few blankets and what looked like a pathetic attempt at a cooking implement.

She picked up a pot. "The only thing you could boil in that is an egg, which you won't find here."

"I just fancied tea at dawn," said Aggie.

"You'll have Dixie's family sniffing around if you do that." She ruffled Dixie's head. "Nosy buggers."

Dixie nuzzled the Alien with a warm grunt.

The Alien gestured a "come this way."

"What about my tent?" said Aggie.

"Pfff, that—the wind will have that by nightfall."

"Oh," said Aggie. "I spent a week's wages on that."

"You were robbed," she said.

Aggie tried to keep up with the Alien called Tork. She staggered behind, clutching her bag, as Tork's young, muscular body weaved through the fields, her flared trousers flapping in the grass.

Beside the path were fields of hemp waving in the wind. Aggie, heady from the scent, began to fixate on Tork's magnificent rolling butt and the tool belt slung across it.

Dixie, ambling beside her, stuck her wet nose into Aggie's face.

"Come on, slapper," shouted Tork.

Aggie stopped. "What did you call me?"

"Slapper. Didn't you slap the leader?"

"No," said Aggie.

"That's not what I heard," said Tork.

"It was *he* who talked of slapping *me*," said Aggie.

Tork, with a "who cares" shrug, carried on.

"Like a mere rug," said Aggie.

"As if," shouted Tork over her shoulder.

Tork lived on her own in the village and was what they called "just starting out." The Aliens lived in huts similar to those the women lived in in the city but with way better shelving.

She tossed Aggie blankets in the corner of her hut and the pot into the communal kitchen, setting off a series of laughter and head-patting for Aggie.

The village welcomed her for breakfast with a seat next to Tork. They sat outside by a long wooden table on bench seats, which rumbled with the odd "breaking of wind" like a dodgy hot water pipe.

Aggie looked about for cutlery, and they started to laugh.

"We use our hands here," said one.

"Yeah," said another, "or is that too good for a slapper?"

"I didn't slap," said Aggie, looking at her chunk of bread.

Tork told her to dunk.

"Can you imagine what would happen if I actually slapped that giant of a man?" said Aggie.

She dipped her bread; it absorbed nothing.

The group stared at her.

"He does pull spaceships, you know . . ." said Aggie.

A few chuckled, some returning to their bread-dipping.

". . . down the main street," added Aggie.

"Oooh, how brave," muttered one.

Aggie eyed her bread.

"You need to do it longer," whispered Tork.

Aggie looked at her.

"The bread . . . dip it in *longer*," said Tork.

"Some say he is a pussy," said an ancient-looking woman known as Cat on account of her catlike eyes.

She held Aggie's gaze, slid the bread into her mouth, and sucked it.

"You shouldn't believe all you hear," snapped Aggie.

"It was a reliable source," Cat mumbled with a mouthful.

No one said anything.

"And my sources are indisputable," said Cat.

"Let's not go there," muttered a voice from the back.

"As reliable as the building they come from," said Cat.

"How 'bout we start clearing up," said another. A few jumped to their feet, piling plates.

"Building?" said Aggie.

Tork hissed a "don't go there."

"The library," said Cat.

The women groaned.

"Library?" said Aggie. "Just because it comes out of the library doesn't mean it's . . . well . . . worth anything."

The women stopped, staring at Aggie.

"The Library is the fountain of all things," snapped Cat.

"It's just a building," chuckled Aggie, "run by an idiot."

Cat spat out her bread, eyeballing Aggie.

"Full of writings, tables, and . . . *books*," she said.

"So?" said Aggie.

The women gasped.

"But reading is everything," snapped Cat.

"That depends on the book *and* the reader," said Aggie.

The two women glared at each other.

"Time for the dishes," jumped in a large woman called Maisie.

---

1. *A bit like the Australian outback, but without kangaroos.*

Chapter Twenty-Four

BREAKFAST

"There is more to drying dishes than a tea towel."–The Washerwoman

*A*ggie hadn't even left the city and James the Strong was already regretting the loss.

The morning she left, he walked into the meeting room, aimless and confused, and caught LM-2 on her own. She stopped and turned, and as sunlight caught her profile, he realized why he felt so aroused by her side.

Why had he not seen her before?

"She's gone," he said.

LM-2 nodded.

"I have set her free," he lied.

"So I heard," she lied.

He caught her eye.

She said nothing.

He gazed at her body, taking in every inch, stopping at her cap.

"Why the cap inside?" he whispered.

"I hate wigs," she murmured.

He smiled. "Me too."

❖

Aggie was thrown into the kitchen for cleanup duty. She, mid bread-sucking, was slung over the shoulder of Maisie and deposited like a sack of soya beans by the sink.

In fact, that was what she was called: a "woozy sack of soya."

Aggie with no idea how soya could be woozy was about to ask when a tea towel was tossed at her with a "dry" command.

Aggie, gulping the last of her bread, scraped the towel from her face.

Dry, she thought and looked for someone to copy. There was no one in the shed-like kitchen; it was empty except for equipment as foreign to Aggie as a Victorian corset.

Manifesto the Strong tugged at LM-2's cap. It fell to the ground, revealing a glistening blond bun at the top of her head. He moved closer and inhaled the scent of her hair.

LM-2's heart raced.

She had heard of his past, his ability to reduce a woman to a wreck of sighs and moans. She told herself she would not be one of them, that she was a Foreigner first and a woman second.

She made a halfhearted attempt to replace her cap, but as soon as he touched her hair, she was gone, and as her locks tumbled, so did her resolve.

Manifesto the Strong moved in for the kill, his family member rising to the occasion like the swell of perfectly baked bread.

The sun burst through the clear ceiling of the kitchen, giving Aggie a perfect view of a room built for a purpose of which she had no idea.

She stared at the plates, pots, and pans piled by the sink, the walls covered in a masterpiece of shelving, the large table in the middle, and wondered, *What the pickling shag am I to do?*

The women were outside acting like she was invisible. She could see them scraping their plates into large bins by the expansive garage-like entrance.

They were nothing like the women she knew. They had arms like dumbbells and low voices that purred. They walked and marched like men, shoving each other and cracking jokes at a moment's notice.

Tork, on hot water duty, was by the fire lifting buckets of the stuff like she was picking flowers. Aggie caught sight of her lifting her top over her head with the sort of muscular arms she had only seen on James the Strong.

Tork's brown skin glistened under the sun, her whisper of a vest exposing a taut torso with a hint of a nipple. Aggie stared. For a moment, she felt something she hadn't felt in years—a yearning to touch.

Tork caught her eye, flashed a white smile, then waltzed into the kitchen with a bucket and emptied it into the sink like it was a teacup.

Steam filled the kitchen.

Another older woman appeared, took up her station at the sink, eyed the pile of dishes, and sunk her hands into the hot water.

Aggie waited for instructions.

I'm not a mind reader, she thought.

"You soon will be," snapped the Washerwoman, "now dry."

The women outside roared with laughter, some slapping each other on the back.

Aggie lifted her towel and looked about.

"The plates," said Tork with a kind face.

Aggie lifted a plate; a rat clutching a lump of bread stared back.

Aggie jumped, screamed . . . and dropped the plate. The crash blasted through the eating area.

The rat screamed, bread crumbs spewing from its mouth like a burst pipe.

Aggie yelped as spit-covered crumbs splattered onto her face and stuck fast.

The rat, still clutching its bread, scurried as Aggie, with another shriek, realized the tail was left behind.

Tork chuckled, clutching her stomach.

A woman emptying the bins laughed her head off.

"Don't mind Toby," she shouted, wiping tears of laughter. "That rat keeps the garbage at bay."

LM-2 stared into the dark; it was a full moon, and she felt fantastic. She had no idea of such pleasure. She looked at James the Strong, ran her finger along his giant of a nose, and sighed.

All her life, LM-2 had lived under the shadow of her grandfather. She never knew a man who'd managed to needle his way into the favor of Wife-ie. Her father wanted a boy to follow in Loud Mouth's foot-steps—he even dressed LM-2 as one, until her mother put her foot down and stopped all bed-diving.

Well, look at me now, Dad, she thought.

Then she blushed; perhaps it was better he didn't.

Chapter Twenty-Five

CAT

"A slap on the back is better than a slap in the face."–Tork

*a*n hour and several rats later, Aggie had the whole drying thing down to a fine art, and as she piled the last of the plates into the corner, she waited for a "cheers," a "thanks," maybe even a "well done" and a slap on the back.

The Washerwoman looked at her. "Drying dishes is not exactly rocket science," she said.

"Well yes, I know, but . . ." Aggie faltered. "I did get a nice shine on them."

"Shine?" yelled a woman from outside. "Who gives a flying pickle about a shine?"

The women outside, having cleared the table, were sitting around plotting the day, arguing over who *should* do what with whom and who *had* done nothing and should be ashamed of themselves, occasionally bursting into a fight and just as quickly laughing.

"You'll need to get cracking," yelled Maisie.

"Cracking?" said Aggie.

"You've the fields to do," sniggered another, shoving Maisie off her chair.

"To be done before elevenses," shouted the Washerwoman.

"Elevenses?" said Aggie.

"That's right," said Cat. "Tea break's at eleven."

"You want *me* to go into the fields?" said Aggie.

"If you want feed, you need to earn it," shouted the shover.

"We'll have none of your hoity-toity city malarkey here," said the Washerwoman.

The women outside laughed, and they laughed even louder when the Washerwoman gestured to the highest shelf.

"And you'll need to put them dishes out of the rats' reach first."

Aggie stared up to the high ceiling. *Ten shelves?* She gulped. "To the top?"

Tork pulled out a ladder hidden under a shelf with a "here."

"On those?" said Aggie.

"What do you think you're gonna do? Fly up?" yelled Maisie, shoving the shover.

Aggie stared down at the rickety ladder.

"Hurry up, they won't move 'emselves," snapped the Washerwoman.

Tork told her not to worry, that the steps were stronger than they looked.

Aggie slid her foot on the first rung, and Tork grabbed her waist with an "I've got you" whisper.

Aggie could've stayed all day with Tork's hand on her waist and was just thinking of something witty to say in reply when the Washerwoman turned to the women outside.

"Just need one more bucket of water and I'm done here."

"I'm on it," said Cat.

Aggie stopped. "Her? Buckets of water?"

Cat stood from her seat. Her small hobbitlike body barely changed in height.

"She's old," said Aggie. "Ancient."

"So?" said the Washerwoman.

"One puff of wind and she'll be over," said Aggie.

"There's no wind," said the Washerwoman.

"She walks with a stick," said Aggie.

"So?" said the Bin Emptier.

"How is she to carry a bucket?"

Cat slid her stick onto her belt and rubbed her hands with a "get ready, girls . . ."

The women started to cheer.

Bent double like a turtle, Cat shuffled to the fire. Her cloak dragged on the ground and she stumbled; Maisie steadied her with an "easy."

"Is that safe, her walking in that thing?" said Aggie.

"Safe? Of course it's safe," snapped the Washerwoman.

"But she just tripped," said Aggie.

Cat stopped at the fire. She reached for a bucket, faltered, took a breath, and looked at her audience.

"You can do it," shouted a voice from the back.

"She's not going to lift a bucket . . ." Aggie looked at Tork. "Is she?"

"Of course," said Tork.

"Naturally," said the Washerwoman.

"One bucket or two?" shouted Cat.

"When is one enough?" yelled Tork.

"Two?" said Aggie.

"Make it three," shouted the Washerwoman.

"Three?" said Aggie. "What is she, an octopus?"

Tork and the Washerwoman, having no idea what an octopus was, said nothing. Instead, they chuckled.

"Go on, do your usual head-balancing," said Tork.

Cat, perfecting a Parkinson's shake, reached for the bucket; she stumbled, tripping just shy of the flames. The shover and Maisie grabbed her.

"Steady . . ." said Maisie.

"Third time lucky," croaked Cat with an arthritic reach.

"Let me," yelled Aggie, charging to the fire.

She got within a foot and was knocked back by the heat.

The women cackled, some calling her a pussy.

Aggie, red-faced and sweating, did not give up. Shielding her face, she moved toward the fire and made a grasp for the handle, then instantly jumped back with every swear word she knew while blowing on her now-burnt hand.

Cat, with a "here," pushed Aggie out of the way and effortlessly placed a bucket on her head.

She, now erect as a sergeant with not a shake in sight, stood to a round of applause while two women slid a bucket into each hand.

"Off into the breech." Cat jigged without spilling a drop. Then, as the clapping continued, she sauntered to the kitchen.

Aggie followed behind.

She felt like a fool, and the women jeering at her didn't help. It was like she was a child again, alone in the corner, the butt of jokes and everyone laughing at her.

Tork slapped her on the back, almost knocking her for six.

"Don't worry, you're not the first to be fooled. A week in the field will have your hands as hard as this here Washerwoman's."

Aggie, blowing on her hands, said nothing. *A child could have done better than me,* she thought, then stopped. She looked around. *Where are the children? Come to think of it, where are the men?*

She nudged Tork. "Are the others in the fields?"

"Others?" said the Washerwoman.

"The children?" said Aggie.

The laughing stopped; women gasped.

The Washerwoman glared at Aggie and snapped, "It's time for you to head to the field."

Aggie spent her days working the fields in trousers and a top made of hemp cloth that flapped about her thin body until she sweated enough for it to stick.

She, like the rest, went commando, which, according to Tork, "made alfresco toileting a breeze."

It took her a day to get used to squatting and several more to adjust to the itchy material, which under the burning sun absorbed her sweat.

Every bit of her body ached.

Her stomach growled, her hips throbbed, and her hands were covered with sores and hacks, and yet there was something satisfying about the hard work, and she knew, despite being ignored, that it was only a matter of time before she was accepted. She just had to find out what they were hiding from her.

Every night by the campfire, they handed her their so-called "tea," and every morning, she woke with no memory of finishing the tea or how she got into bed.

Aggie, with a belly full of stew, would watch as the women laughed, joked, and argued, wondering when the men would arrive. The women argued over everything from crop rotations to rat tail recycling to trading, and a fight always broke out.

The next thing she knew, it was morning, she was staring at the ceiling in Tork's hut, and Tork, standing nearby, was clutching a mug with a "this'll put a pep in your step" and a smile.

Tork always told her not to tell the others; they'd call her "soft."

And before Aggie had managed an "Arrrrh," the warm liquid had reached down to her toes and she was bouncing out of bed.

Chapter Twenty-Six

SUFFRAGETTES

"Harlot: a six-letter word that raises more than eyebrows."–
James the Strong

A week later

*W*hile Aggie was learning about living with no underpants, LM-2 was learning about bed-diving and how big a family member could grow.

Within a week, she had mastered many things that would make her mother blush and learnt to manipulate like a real pro. Convincing James the Strong that calling women "harlots" was a bad idea took a mere flick of a hand, a look, and, of course, timing.

"Are you sure?" said James the Strong.

"Did your father ever use such a term?" said LM-2.

James the Strong stared at the ceiling with a screwed-up face, then turned to LM-2.

"Even for those so-called suffragettes who have tea parties?"

LM-2 looked at her lover. "Suffragettes?"

"Yes," said James the Strong. "They toast their tea to the brave women on earth. The Librarian says if any women should be called a harlot, it's them."

LM-2 stopped. "The Librarian? He is but a mere bookkeeper with silly wigs," she muttered. "Shouldn't he be sorting books, stamping dates?"

"Especially this Fanny," said James the Strong. He fingered LM-2's collarbone, working his way down . . . "The Librarian has even set up talks with Fanny's owner."

"Talks?" snapped LM-2. "What is he, the prime minister?"

James the Strong laughed at his delicious little LM-2.

"Told the owner it was his civic duty to lock her up." He stopped, gazed at her pink nipples. "Or was it lock her down?"

"Lock down a woman?" said LM-2.

She covered herself up.

James the Strong kissed her neck with a "hmmm."

She stroked his hair, letting her fingers linger . . .

"Darling . . ." she whispered, "isn't it you who does the talking?"

James the Strong chuckled. "The Librarian said you'd say that."

"Did he?"

"He said, 'Beware a woman of ideas, especially one pretending to be a man.'"

She uncovered her breast. "Well, I'm not pretending now, am I?"

James the Strong moaned, pulling her under him.

LM-2 eased her pelvis into place, looked into his eyes, and decided to investigate this Fanny and her suffragette tea party . . .

The Librarian listened from one of Aggie's spy holes, completely pissed off. All his hard work, thrown to the wind like yesterday's sperm. He had managed to get rid of one pain-in-the-arse woman just to have a younger model fill her shoes, and from what he could hear, she was even better at manipulating.

He cursed himself for not spotting sooner, for not getting rid of her, for playing it all wrong—yet again.

The talking stick[1] was passed around the fire, ignored by everyone except Aggie. She clung to it, hoping for a chance to be heard.

They hadn't eaten since elevenses and were tucking into a soya drink, waiting for the Washerwoman and her stew to arrive. The hemp tea was kept for later, when stomachs were full; drinking hemp on an empty stomach could "knock a woman senseless."

Aggie was suspicious.

Every night it was the same—lots of this so-called soya drink by the campfire—and the more she drank, the thirstier she felt. The soya drink was as good for quenching a thirst as the talking stick for talking; in fact, she was sure it was spiked.

What else would have her like a zombie after one mug, waking up with no idea how she'd gotten to her bed?

Well, not tonight, she told herself. Things are going to be different. She discreetly emptied her mug.

Thanks to years of sharing a bed with James the Strong, she was a pro at pretending to sleep, and tonight, she was going to pretend her socks off.

It seemed like a year since Aggie had flounced about the library, a decade since she'd hammered on Fanny's door; in fact, it was only a week. Seven days, one the same as the next. The same breakfast, elevenses, jokes, fighting, fieldwork; even the evenings were the same.

The only things different were the spectacular sunsets and sunrises and the names of the four-legged creatures, and of course the fighting.

At some point in the night, a fight would break out—usually when the egg shed was mentioned—which always led to a couple of women rolling around in the dust trying a variety of moves.

Every night, Aggie watched and waited, wondering when the men would arrive, forgetting as soon as a top was ripped, a muscle flexed; then she, like the rest, egged the wrestlers on.

In those moments of glistening skin and firelight, Aggie felt alive, like she had years ago when she first bed-dived—until, that is, the so-called soya drink sent her to sleep . . .

Aggie wondered what James the Strong would have made of it all. She suspected he'd have fit right in like the rats in the kitchen.

She tried to tell Tork about her past life, but Tork seemed to know before she said anything. In fact, most of them did. How they knew anything was a mystery to her; they didn't read, hardly listened, and yet it was like they knew what she was going to say before she spoke.

Until she talked of men.

"Men?" snapped Maisie.

"Men?" muttered a few in the back.

"We're as good as men," said the shover.

The women nodded.

"But you're not men, you're women . . ." said Aggie.

The women gasped. Some looked away, others glared at her.

". . . aren't you?" said Aggie.

"All in good time, dear," muttered the Bin Emptier, ruffling Aggie's hair like she was another Dixie.

Aggie huffed, fed up.

She had a right to ask to be told things. *She* had *brains,* could sort things—help—but all she got was "dear" this and "dear" that, airy-fairy comments about "initiation" and the "egg shed," and her head rubbed like she was a two-legged Dixie.

She watched as the Washerwoman plunked her pot of stew in the middle of the circle.

"The truth is, we don't need 'em anymore," said the Washerwoman.

"Need men? Everyone needs men. I mean, they *can* be pretty annoying and stupid," said Aggie.

"Stupid? Who you calling stupid," snapped a voice from the back.

Aggie laughed. "But they can be manipulated."

"That's why you're here then, cause you're so good at manipulating?" said the shover.

"Well, I . . ." Aggie stopped. "What about babies, offspring?"

"You don't want to know much, do you?" snapped Cat.

"It's not much to want to know where babies come from," muttered Aggie.

"Let's just leave it, shall we?" said the Washerwoman, thrusting a plate of vegetables under Aggie's nose as Maisie, with a side glance at her comrades, filled Aggie's mug with a "drink up."

Aggie glanced around at the faces waiting for her to drink. What she needed was a diversion . . .

❖

"In the city, they say you worship hemp," said Aggie.

"And what's wrong with that?" huffed the Bin Emptier.

"That there's dancing . . ." said Aggie.

"Pfff, you see us dancing?" said the shover.

"Crazy drumming that sends folk into a trance," said Aggie.

"Like they know what they're talking about," muttered a voice from the back.

"Wild women beating men with talking sticks," said Aggie, now making things up.

Maisie ripped the talking stick from Aggie. "Told you, we don't talk of men."

"They're like the talking stick," Tork laughed. "Useless."

"Why don't you drink up?" said the shover to Aggie.

"Here, have some hemp—knock yourself out," muttered the Washerwoman.

Aggie sighed. She now had two mugs to empty . . .

---

1. *Passed around like a good old fashion fag. The holding of the stick meant you had the floor and could "talk the hind leg of a flour legged creature," "ad infinitum," except some took the "ad infinitum" literally, leading to the tossing of said talking stick.*

   In the end, the talking stick became as obsolete as arm wrestling, finding a home in the museum of field workers, a museum with no entrance fee as there is bugger all to see.

Chapter Twenty-Seven

PUTTY IN HER HANDS

"Thanks to sunrises, you never know what you're gonna wake up to."—Tork

A rat passed Aggie's foot; she held her breath, trying not to move. It wiggled up her leg, under her top, and nibbled her belly button.

She froze, then let out a loud snore . . .

"That was quick," muttered Maisie.

"Eye, too quick," muttered Cat.

"Probably your knock-knock jokes," said the Bin Emptier.

Aggie affected a roll. The rat, annoyingly, went with it, zigzagging higher.

Aggie started to sweat.

The rat skidded on her skin.

She let out a loud James the Strong snore.

The rat jumped, scratching her skin, and scurried to her shoulder . . .

She stifled a scream.

Aggie had managed to empty her mugs with not a drop of liquid touching her lips, and now, feigning sleep like in the good old James the Strong days, she was beginning to regret it.

She had used every diversion she could think of, and when that didn't work, she threw in a stupid knock-knock joke, sending the Aliens into a chorus of groans—apart from the Bin Emptier.

She, jumping in with her famed "egg-static" joke, sparked of a series of slapping and shoving while some shouted, "Hemp effluent."

Aggie emptied one mug, then the other as the Bin Emptier challenged the shover to an arm wrestle.

Aggie hadn't counted on the rat.

It scrambled across her cheek, she feigned a "nightmare" toss and turn, shouting "get off me!"

Tork looked at her. "I don't know why you need to put her out like that."

"She was asking too many questions," said the Washerwoman, "so I gave her extra."

The rat, clinging onto her ear, began to nibble.

Aggie almost wet herself.

"Extra what?" said Cat.

"Hemp," said the Washerwoman.

A few whistled through their teeth.

"On an empty stomach?" said Maisie.

"For pickle's sake, she'll have a head like a thundercloud," snapped Tork, slapping the rat away. The tail flopped onto Aggie's neck.

"She can't be trusted," said a voice from the back.

"She passed the 'old git' test the first morning," said Tork. "How much more do you need?"

"A mere ploy," said the Washerwoman.

The others laughed.

"Those city folk are good with ploys," said the shover.

"And she's privileged," said the Washerwoman. "Never seen a tea towel in her life."

"So?" said Tork.

"She's a wuss," shouted the voice from the back.

Wuss? thought Aggie.

"Right—girlie," said the voice from the back.

Girlie? thought Aggie. *What's that when it's slathered on bread?*

"They all are in that city trying to trap men," said the shover.

"I think it is the men that trap them," muttered Tork, flicking the tail from Aggie's cheek.

Aggie thought of the things she knew, the things she'd done. *I have organized, argued, and bed-dived, all for the good of this pickling planet . . . and they call me a* wuss?

"I miss being a man," muttered a voice.

Aggie stopped . . .

"I miss being a woman," muttered another.

Aggie held her breath . . .

"I can't remember what I was," said the voice from the back.

Aggie listened as the Aliens began to slur their words.

"If only I were a man again, I'd think straight," said the shover.

"I thought you were a woman," said Maisie.

"I'm sure I had a set of balls," said the shover.

A few sniggered.

"You sure she's not listening?" said Cat.

Aggie let out a snore.

"Nah, she's snoring," muttered Maisie.

"Never snored before," muttered Cat.

"It's the hemp," said the Washerwoman. "Told you, I gave her extra."

"Still, you'd better move her; the last thing we need is her blabbing," said Cat.

"To whom is she gonna blab?" huffed Tork. "Dixie over there?"

Maisie scooped up Aggie with a grunt as Aggie made like a cat and flopped.

"She's out of it tonight. How much hemp did you give her?" groaned Maisie.

"Enough," said the Washerwoman.

Tork and Maisie laid Aggie onto her bed. Tork tenderly tucked a blanket around Aggie, while Maisie, with one of her annoying head pats, shouted,

"We could use her."

"What?" said Tork.

"For the shed," Maisie yelled.

"For pickle's sake," huffed Tork. "We should at least ask."

Maisie looked down at Aggie's smooth face.

"Her eggs are probably still good," she shouted. "Her skin's still smooth."

My eggs? thought Aggie.

"What good is an egg without a seed?" yelled the Washerwoman, and before any could answer, Cat butted in . . .

"Come away from there," she hissed. "Folk hear things in their sleep."

Aggie heard everything. She listened as the hemp tea slurred their tongues, and when they finally staggered off to bed, she was more confused than ever.

Some talked of a future and having "a lot to decide," others shouted that they "had none" and that they were just going to "die out."

While the Bin Emptier talked of the "great hemp god."

"Will you stop it with the hemp? It's just a seed, some grass," said the Washerwoman.

"But look what the hemp has given us," said the Bin Emptier. "Life, happiness, laughter, and four-legged friends."

"Yes, but it hasn't given us back our balls, has it?" said Maisie.

"It gave us the egg shed," said the Bin Emptier.

"I think you'll find we built that," said the Washerwoman.

The next morning, Aggie sat outside the hut and watched the sun rise with a head as clear as the waterfall water. She pulled the "underground" cards from her pocket and shuffled them between her fingers.

Everyone knew about Fanny's tea parties, but an underground? She had no idea what an underground was, but she had heard of the women's discontentment, rumblings of wanting more . . .

When she heard Tork's "I'm awake" cough, she headed inside, made two caffeines, sat on Tork's bed, and looked into her face.

Who was she at one time, a man or a woman?

Tork opened her eyes and looked straight into Aggie's.

"I was a woman," she said.

"How do you do that?" said Aggie.

"What?" said Tork.

"Read my mind?"

Tork touched her face. "You talk in your sleep."

LM-2 decided to investigate *this* "Fanny." The easiest way to do this was to dress as a boy and head into the streets.

She found out many things . . .

That most men had no idea of Fanny and her suffragette tea parties, and that those who did didn't care.

That, despite some women claiming the tea "undrinkable" and the dress code "insufferable," the number of women was growing, and that suffragette leaflets could be found in the only place men never ventured—kindergartens.

LM-2, braving the noise, headed in, and before she could shoo a child from her knee, a leaflet was thrust in her face.

Chapter Twenty-Eight

THE SHED

"'Hermaphrodites'—a long word for 'sitting on the fence.'" James the Strong

"Tell me about the egg shed," said Aggie.

Tork sipped her caffeine. "You're not ready."

Aggie threw her a look.

"Besides, you have to be initiated."

Aggie threw her another look.

"Which is more arm wrestling than anything else."

Aggie waited.

"Maisie came up with the idea."

Aggie sipped her caffeine.

The scent of Tork lingered. It was the sort of scent that made Aggie smile, her pinched face a distant memory.

She wanted to help; she knew she could. She just hadn't worked out how . . .

"I think she was bored," said Tork. She stopped, looked at Aggie. "Did you drink *any* of that tea last night?"

Aggie shook her head. "Not a drop—I heard everything."

"I thought the snoring was over the top," muttered Tork. She sighed. "I suppose I could take you there."

Aggie smiled at her.

"But . . . you must promise not to say anything," said Tork.

"Absolutely," Aggie said, nodding like a first-class politician.

She followed Tork through a lush green field where the four-legged creatures were fattened up for those in the city. She fingered the underground cards in her pocket, toying with the idea of asking Tork, who seemed to know everything.

"Tork," she said, "what's an underground?"

Tork, without hearing, pointed to a line of run-down sheds.

Aggie's heart sank. She was expecting something metallic, shiny, like a stationary spaceship, not something you'd store a lawn mower in.

Tork marched on, ignoring her. "Is that it?"

Aggie watched Tork wrestle with the wonky door, jiggling the key inside the lock, and was just on the verge of shouting "Why don't you just kick it down?" when the door creaked open.

Aggie stared inside, expecting a rustic pile of equipment along with perhaps a dog-eared manual—and rats.

She stared into the dark.

Hmmmmm . . .

Bubble-bubble . . . buzz . . .

Hmmmm . . .

Tork marched in.

Aggie gingerly followed.

The door clicked shut behind her.

She turned . . .

The lights flashed on.

She gasped and stared . . .

In front of her was a labyrinth of shelves, vast and complicated, filled with test tubes and jars, pulsating with energy.

There was not a rat's tail in sight.

"Your kitchen's shelving is a mere bookcase compared to this," Aggie muttered.

"I know," said Tork.

"It's like the nurturing shed," said Aggie, "and yet so much more."

"Nurturing?" Tork looked at her. "We use this for home brew and hemp tea."

Aggie ran her fingers along the shiny surfaces. "They call it the

Institute now," she said. She lifted a test tube and sniffed. "James the Strong tried to shut it down once."

Tork told her not to touch . . .

"It was the needles, put the boss off," muttered Aggie.

She opened a glass jar and pulled a face.

Tork took the jar from her and closed it.

"James the Strong couldn't see past the prick." She turned to Tork. "Needles are the future, I told him, along with Petri dishes."

Aggie picked up a basket of fungi.

"You need a white coat to do that," Tork said.

Aggie dropped the basket and moved to the door where several hung.

"And permission," said Tork.

Aggie stopped. "Permission?"

"It is a complicated process, you know—you do need training," said Tork.

Aggie poked her nose into a fridge. "For making tea?"

"Yes, and . . . well . . . other things."

"Hmm, looks like lots of other things," muttered Aggie.

She lifted a bottle with Tork's name on it and jiggled what looked like marbles.

"There was a time . . . when we tried to, err . . . fertilize our eggs here," muttered Tork.

Aggie stopped. "Eggs?"

"Yes, eggs—they were the first to go," said Tork. "Then it was the seed."

Aggie slid the bottle back into the fridge.

"At first, the slow-growing soya was enough, but as the city grew, we couldn't keep up the supply. We had to improve on things, design better soya. By the time we realized what working with this new soya did to us, it was too late.

Aggie thought of James the Strong. *He was addicted to the stuff,* had it *on everything. The Librarian said it was good for bones.*

"It was the arm wrestling that gave it away," said Tork. "Suddenly, the women were winning as much as the men. Then the men changed, began to huddle in corners, grow breasts, and disappear for days. It was the Washerwoman who built this to store our seeds and eggs, but," said Tork, "it was too late; we'd morphed into, well . . . what we are now. Everything's sterile, and we're neither man nor woman . . ."

Aggie eyed Tork's muscular legs, rocklike breasts, and strong hands. "But you call yourselves women," she said.

"Cat's idea. She's a bit of a soothsayer," said Tork.

"Does she have extra sight?" said Aggie.

"No, just reads," said Tork. "When she was a trader, she traded for books. Her hut is full of them. She says that soon, the planet will be full of women and bugger-all men, apart from the odd footmen."

"Pfff, as if," laughed Aggie.

After a particularly aerobic night of bed-diving, LM-2 eased herself out from under James the Strong.

He was comatose, his family member as empty as a squeezed lemon, and as she slid his tree trunk of a thigh onto the bed, she told herself she had all night.

She pulled on her boy's outfit, slid her hair under a cap, and, with a soft look at James the Strong, slipped into the night.

Chapter Twenty-Nine

THE UNDERGROUND

"There are only two ways a woman manipulates a man, and one is via children."—The Beverage Maker

The underground was held in the Foreigners' spaceship, a place which, according to Fanny, was perfect for meetings, as no man ventured near the ship and it had excellent catering facilities.

Fanny, wearing her favorite easy-to-wipe Teflon take on a suffragette dress, opened the door and, catching sight of LM-2's cap, nearly shut it again, until LM-2 spoke.

The arrival of LM-2 changed everything.

Her disguise impressed them all, apart from Fanny. Then, when they found out who her partner was, they swooned—*what a coup.*

"She's the top of the tree," said the Beverage Maker.

"I wouldn't say top," muttered Fanny's Sidekick. "Our Fanny is the top."

The women turned to LM-2, waiting for a response.

"Revolution is not about old positions," muttered Fanny.

"Positions? She's shagging the leader," said the Warden. "Positions are her cornerstone."

LM-2 shifted uncomfortably.

"We don't talk of shagging here," muttered the Sidekick.

"Well, thanks to her 'shagging,' things are gonna be a hell of a lot easier for the rest of us," said the warden.

"We don't talk of hell either," said the Sidekick.

"We do where I come from," said the Poet.

The Sidekick threw a "don't we know it" look at the Poet.

"My job is to record for all perpetuity, and hell is a fair part of that," said the Poet.

No one listened.

"The pen is mightier than the sword," she said.

"So is shagging, but you don't hear *her* banging on about it," muttered the Sidekick.

LM-2 blushed.

Fanny stood up. "We need to discuss weapons."

"Nothing gets past my pen," continued the Poet. She turned to LM-2. "Tell me about your exploits—where has all this shagging got you?"

LM-2's face stiffened.

"There is more to me than shagging," she snapped.

"It's your greatest tool," said the Warden.

"You would know," said a voice from the back. "You've shagged every reader going."

"Comrades, please," said Fanny.

The Poet nudged LM-2. "Tell us, is he as big as we are led to believe?"

"There is more to me than a vagina," snapped LM-2.

The women gasped at the word.

"I have a brain."

"A Foreigner with a brain?" muttered the voice from the back.

"It was me who developed switches on mirrors."

"That was you?" said Fanny.

"Yes. They thought I was a boy . . . let me work alongside men, designing, inventing—all that sort of thing."

Silence.

"In fact, we're working on mechanical birds to address the wasp situation."

A few nodded.

"Although I'm not entirely convinced mechanical is the way to go," said LM-2.

"Do you know anything about bras?" said Fanny.

"Bras?" said LM-2 with a quizzical look.

The women groaned.

"We are not turning our bras into weapons," snapped the Beverage Maker, poised by the caffeine machine.

"It will take them by surprise," said Fanny.

"Surprise?" muttered the voice from back with a fair amount of face pulling.

"Well, I for one love my bra," snapped the Beverage Maker.

A few of the women nodded.

"And my bra is remaining firmly where it is," said the Beverage Maker, thrusting a mug under the frother. "You may like a corset, but I am sticking with the underwire."

LM-2 watched as the voluptuous Beverage Maker frothed with vigor. She had never seen tea made like that before.

The Poet nudged LM-2.

"That stuff gets me through the meetings. Agreeing in this place is as probable as your James the Strong sticking to one woman."

"Thanks," muttered LM-2.

After several cups of roasted caffeine beans, LM-2's mind was whirling. She had spent so much time in the company of men she had forgotten what it was like to be with women.

They were all over the place, she thought. Hung up on too many issues . . .

Fanny's militant style didn't help; it was wearing thinner than her petticoat, particularly her talk on the hidden powers of the underwire. No one listened.

"We just want a break," said the Poet. "I'm fed up feeding and breeding—I want to do other things."

"Me too," said the beverage maker, handing around the caffeine. "I want to climb a mountain. I hear there are a few outside the city."

The women sipped.

"Arrrrh . . ."

"We want freedom to choose," yelled Fanny.

The women nodded.

"Who to be with," said Fanny.

"*And* over our bits and pieces," muttered the voice from the back.

The Sidekick turned to LM-2. "It's not that we have anything against children."

"No, not at all," said the voice from the back.

"It's just that one is enough."

"Two at a push."

"And a little childcare wouldn't go amiss."

"Help with cleaning," slurped the voice from the back. "And don't get me started on the toilet seat."

The women nodded.

"Oh, absolutely."

"I mean what that's about?" muttered the Beverage Maker.

"Is a lid not for putting down?" quoted the Poet. "A brush not for brushing?"

"The times I have asked," muttered the Beverage Maker. "Like pissing in the wind."

The women chuckled.

"And freedom requires weapons . . ." said Fanny.

"Please don't start that again," sighed the Warden.

"Weapons of mass destruction," said Fanny.

"She's obsessed with weapons," muttered the warden. "In fact, if it wasn't for this here caffeine, I'd bugger off, start my own underground —there're a couple of other spaceships to choose from."

"The suffragettes talked of such things," yelled Fanny.

"The suffragettes talked of voting," muttered the warden.

"Voting?" said LM-2.

"It's all those suffragettes talk of. Do you not watch the mirror?" said the Beverage Maker, handing LM-2 a cup.

"I am a tad busy," said LM-2.

The women looked unimpressed.

"It's not easy, manipulating a leader."

"*Manipulating*—is that what you call it?" laughed a voice from the back.

A few chuckled.

"I *did* address the harlot-calling," snapped LM-2.

The women looked at her.

LM-2's face flushed with anger.

"You try designing switches on a mirror for *all* budgets while dressed like a male—not to mention talking like one."

"Only asked," muttered the Beverage Maker.

"There's all that bollocks-scratching, belching, getting stupid jokes about anything remotely phallic, and don't get me started on the 'what I did last night' brag . . ."

"We get the picture," muttered Fanny.

LM-2 huffed. "A man's life is not a woman's life."

The women eyed LM-2 like she was from another planet.

"It's important that we are equal," said Fanny.

"Equal, that's a laugh," muttered LM-2.

"*And*," yelled Fanny, "equality requires weapons of . . . mass destruction."

"Not the underwire again," snapped the critic.

"Who cares about equality? I just want a day to myself," muttered the voice from the back.

"And to sleep all night," muttered the Sidekick.

"Just asking for things doesn't help," said Fanny. "Those who lead can give and take at a whim. We need representation—to speak for ourselves."

LM-2 looked at Fanny in a new light.

"She has a point," she muttered.

No one heard.

❖

It was early morning by the time LM-2 snuck back to her bedroom with a tray of tea for Himself.

LM-2 entered the bedroom, acting like she had been beside her lover all night.

James the Strong rubbed his eyes and looked at his sweetheart; things began to stir beneath the bed.

"You fancy a bit of bed-diving?" he said.

She sighed . . . and slid in beside him.

Chapter Thirty

BREAKFAST REBEL

"They invited us in, only to herd us to the outlands like four-legged creatures. Farming—that saved us."–Cat

The story of the Aliens' arrival and escape had been handed down by the bonfire late at night when the hemp took hold.

Cat saw it as her duty to keep the story alive—how the Aliens expected a welcome and got anything but.

"We didn't even know what an Alien was until they started calling us one," Cat often said. "There we were, looking out of the spaceship expecting a cup of tea, and we were charged at like a flock of winged beasts. It was *they* who gave *us* directions—invited us, then pushed us out. Pickling bastards."

The women had heard the stories many times. Once Cat reverted to "bastards," they knew it was time to pack up the hemp.

"Picking bastards" led to a whole night of storytelling, which the women knew word for word.

"Cat can be a real downer when stoned," muttered Tork to Aggie.

Aggie didn't hear.

She had spent an hour in the shed surveying the shelves . . . now she was marching back for breakfast in her annoyingly determined way that had Tork panicking. Aggie was quietly making plans, which led Tork to assume the worse.

"Don't go thinking you can change things," said Tork.

"But they want my eggs," said Aggie.

"That's just Maisie's effluent ramblings," muttered Tork. "Once she's had a few hemps, she's full of it, worse than old Cat." Tork feigned a laugh. "At least Cat makes sense."

"What you need is a room with books, knowledge, and places to experiment, hide secrets," said Aggie.

"Absolutely," said Tork with no idea how she would ever pull that off.

"Seriously, a library would be the making of this place."

Tork stopped. "Library? Did you say library?"

Aggie carried on walking.

"Whatever you do—don't mention library."

Aggie said nothing. She was too full of hope. The shed was full of it —all that science—and when Tork explained what an underground was, she saw a future of networking and building, the making of something better than fields and huts. A place she could bring her son to. She was even prepared to give her eggs for that hope. All she needed were those boxes she had stored away in the library, a few Petri dishes, and some needles and she'd be laughing.

She fingered the "underground" cards in her pocket; it was all so *possible*.

"I mean it," said Tork.

"Hmm. OK."

"Cat's got a thing about libraries," said Tork. "Reckons they're the bees knees—she'll never shut up."

"Fine."

"She'll drive the women crazy," said Tork.

She stopped. "You're not listening, are you?"

"Of course I am," muttered Aggie.

"Look, those women have long memories of broken promises," said Tork. "They can turn as quick as milk under the sun, and if you think *that* stinks . . ."

Tork watched Aggie march into the breakfast area.

"Shit," she muttered.

❖

LM-2, lying next to a slumbering James the Strong, stared at the ceiling, thinking of Fanny and her bras.

She turned to the large bay window; their bedroom was so high up she could see past the waterfall to the hills.

Pondering the mechanics of an underwire weapon, she counted the early-morning four-legged creatures frolicking and stopped.

The Poet was right . . .

"I used to look out my window and see a sea of four-legged creatures," she claimed. "Now there's just a puddle."

Most of the women laughed at her, claiming there was "plenty of meat," but most of the women at the meeting were either Settlers or Incomers, women attached to wealthy men who "ordered in" their meat. The Foreign women, like the Poet and the Warden, were a mere handful, poor and overworked, so busy they took it in turn to attend the underground, covering each other's shifts.

"Try getting a decent bit of leg on the market," said the Warden.

"That market is a cesspit," muttered a voice from the back. "Even the rats avoid it. That's why we're overrun with wasps."

"Propaganda bollocks," said Fanny.

The women looked at her.

"It's not the market that has caused the plague of wasps, it's that the birds have long gone."

Fanny eyeballed her silent audience.

She loved animals as much as she loved the suffragettes, so much so that she had a garden full of them: birdlike creatures with huge tails, squawking at the sunrise until her man threatened to shoot them.

"It's all that endless celebrating men insist on," she said.

No one said anything.

"The whole carcass-spinning-over-a-fire ritual."

"You're talking of barbecues," said a voice from the back.

"They have burnt more birds than Foreigners make wigs," said Fanny. "And don't get me started on the four-legged creatures."

Fanny, fired up with emotion, paraded the room. "Their numbers are dwindling quicker than the Librarian's hair. It's all this flesh at every meal." She looked at her followers. "Do we really need it? Must we celebrate everything with a throat-slitting?"

"I just look away," muttered a voice from the back.

"You'd think we were cavemen," said Fanny.

"It's sperm-building," said the Beverage Maker.

"There was plenty of that unmentionable stuff on the spaceship, and you didn't see any flesh-burning," snapped Fanny.

"Meat gives me heartburn," muttered the Sidekick.

Fanny turned to her audience.

"If we ruled, there be none of that; we'd have animals frolicking, heaps of manure, and bonfires that smelt of hemp."

The women looked at each other, confused.

"I thought we wanted a vote," muttered one.

"That's just the beginning." Fanny paced. "With weapons of mass destruction, we could take over, create peace."

"But we *have* peace," said the Warden.

"And look what weapons have done: killed the four-legged creatures faster than they can breed," said the Beverage Maker.

For a moment, Fanny was speechless.

LM-2 looked at the bedroom's walls covered in skins . . . the long furry dangly thing that covered James the Strong's family member slung across the chair . . .

There is more skin on these walls than socks in his drawer, thought LM-2.

James the Strong stirred . . . he turned, his eyes fluttered open, and he smiled at his little princess.

She thought of the mechanical bird created to take care of the wasps.

Fanny made sense, apart from the bras . . .

James the Strong traced his fingers along her jaw. "What's my petal thinking that has her so quiet?"

"Underwear," she said.

"Underwear," jolted James the Strong, "is not worth the spelling of so many letters."

"What?" said LM-2.

"Real men like it swinging freely, a bit of air about the family member." James the Strong laughed. "Would you like to see?"

❖

"What you need is a library," shouted Aggie.

They looked up, saw it was Aggie, and resumed their bread-dunking.

"A convoy," shouted Aggie.

They continued to dunk.

Tork's stomach churned like a cement mixer . . .

Aggie pushed a few plates off the table and jumped onto it.

"Here, what are you doing?" snapped the Bin Emptier.

"Get out of it," shouted another.

"A convoy," shouted Aggie, "will sort things."

The women looked at Aggie like she had two heads and five breasts. Where was the hangover, the still-stoned expression? She looked fresh and alert, like she'd had nothing more than water the night before.

It was Cat who first realized she had only pretended to be asleep.

"That's the sort of thing women are good at—getting out of things," she muttered.

"Yes, well, spiking is the sort of thing that *men* do to get *women* to do those things," snapped Aggie.

Cat blushed.

"Get down," hissed Tork.

"If you want my eggs, you're gonna have to listen to me first," yelled Aggie.

"Here, give me your hand," said Tork with a tug.

"Thought you gave her extra hemp," muttered the Bin Emptier.

"Not much good if she didn't take it," said the Washerwoman.

The Bin Emptier stopped. "What a waste of good hemp."

Chapter Thirty-One

PETRI DISHES

"A test tube is not a test tube without a Petri dish."—Aggie

At first, no one listened to Aggie and her "fountain of knowledge" speech. They all knew that offspring were a pipe dream—that a human egg without a seed was as much use as a spade without a foot.

Until Aggie mentioned "Petri dishes."

Maisie, mid bread-dipping, sat up. "What's that when it's at home?"

"A test tube—it's not a test tube without one," said Aggie. "And if we do a raid, we could collect a ton of them."

"Raid the library?" said Cat brightly.

"I thought you said 'convoy,'" muttered a voice from the back.

"We could skip across to the nurturing shed while we're at it," said Aggie.

The shover's jaw dropped. "Skip?"

"There are needles there," said Aggie.

"Oooh, needles," said the Washerwoman, brushing the table.

"All boxed, ready to go . . . nobody wants them. All we need to do is enter the city," said Aggie.

"Well, that's not much of a plan, is it?" said Maisie. "Let alone a convoy."

"More a raid," said a voice from the back. "Collecting stuff we don't need."

"There's plenty of *stuff* in the library worth collecting," said Cat.

"There are a few elements to be fine-tuned," said Aggie, "but essentially—"

"Elements," said the shover, "like why raid in the first place?"

Aggie, tossing her underground cards on the table, talked of a better future and networking.

"There are other women fed up, left, dumped—we could set up a connection. We could *really* make a difference."

The Washerwoman picked up a card and turned it in her hand.

"Pfff . . . *that* Fanny. She wants fewer children, not more."

"I heard she wants to build weapons out of a bra," laughed the Bin Emptier.

A few laughed; others jeered.

Aggie was losing them.

She thought on her feet . . .

"We could nick a spaceship. We could stick it by the campfire— handy in the rain."

"We go in when it's raining," said Maisie.

"We could make a community," said Aggie. "A real go of things, not just sit around all day moaning about lost balls and eggs."

A few choked on their bread . . .

"Here, enough of that talk, we're eating," snapped the Shover.

She tossed her bread at the bin. It bounced off the side, hitting a perched gull . . .

The gull squawked; a few laughed.

Aggie huffed.

"I do know what I am talking about," she said.

Another tossed her bread at the gull.

The gull snapped it up in one gulp.

"I *was* owned by James the Strong," said Aggie.

The gull began to choke.

Aggie looked at Tork.

Tork shrugged.

"Those men will want to fight," shouted Cat. "They love their library."

"Fight?" A few women jumped.

The gull began to gag and splutter.

"And," said Aggie, "I have a template."

"A template for what?" said the shover.

"For fertilization," lied Aggie. "The Petri dish . . . the needles."

Silence.

Cat grabbed the gull, turned it upside down, and slapped its back. The bird, with a squawk, coughed up the bread as the Poet began to mutter about "the hemp gods answering prayers."

"Our own library," sighed Cat, setting the gull free.

The gull, ruffled within an inch of its life, fluttered into the air inches from the Alien's head, depositing the remains of the previous night's pickings on the table below.

A few nights later, an underground meeting was called.

LM-2 arrived to find the women bent over a map, talking of meetups and trading.

LM-2 had spent some time trying to explain to her lover the extinction of species, but getting him to grasp the concept was like trying to get Fanny to focus on weapons without the mention of a bra. James the Strong had as much interest in the environment as he had in why Aggie had gone off bed-diving; as for mechanical birds, he thought it was a wonderful idea. "No more flying shits."

She stared at the women bent over a table of diagrams like mechanics under the hood of a transporter.

"I'm telling you, it's her," muttered the voice from the back.

"Her?"

"*No.*"

"Seriously?"

"Get out of here."

Fanny turned to LM-2. "A new woman has joined the pack."

"Pack?" said LM-2.

"The Aliens have a new member."

"She made it?" said the Warden.

"Who would want to join them?" said LM-2. "I heard they eat with their hands."

"Who do you think?" said the critic.

"Aggie," said the Beverage Maker, handing a mug to LM-2.

"And she's driving them insane with her questions," said the voice from the back.

"Typical," muttered LM-2.

"She has this stupid idea of a needles raid."

"Pfff," muttered the Sidekick.

"Needles?" said LM-2.

The Foreigner met with the Aliens for trading, and the Aliens, despite having sworn not to tell, often did just that.

Trading was something forced onto women, the lowest of work, leading to a bonding of traders and sharing, sometimes a competing of woes.

When they heard of a new woman who asked more questions than an insurance claim, the Foreigner knew exactly who they were talking of, and when word got out of a "trip to the library" and "needle raiding," they knew exactly who was behind it . . .

"You'll need to stop her," said LM-2.

"Stop her?" gasped a few. They glared at her.

LM-2 didn't falter.

"She can't be trusted."

A few nights later, with tools silenced in soya bags swinging from their belts, the Aliens met at the kitchen table for a "debriefing of sneaking-in tactics."

Maisie appeared clutching a spear, which even Tork thought was a little showy.

"Only a moron would raid with a spear," said the shover.

Tork, for a moment, thought they were going to break into a fight until Cat appeared, lugging extra rope and talking of "swinging."

Aggie tried to tell them tools weren't totally necessary, but as Tork pointed out several times, an Alien is not dressed without her tools.

"But you don't even use them in the field," said Aggie.

A comment Tork chose to ignore.

Aggie had a plan, a vision. She wanted to build a community far away from the soya, a place where she could bring up her son.

Tork called it a pipe dream.

"It wouldn't take much," she said. "A few buildings, a veranda or two, some water, and plants—we'll need a lot of plants."

"And the fertilization?" said Tork.

"Oh, that."

"You promised them seeds?" hissed Tork.

Aggie nodded.

"They'll be expecting babies."

Aggie eyed her pal. *She had gotten carried away.*

"There is no template, is there?" said Tork.

Aggie said nothing.

"How could you?" said Tork.

Aggie looked away.

"We *just* get used to the way of things—adapted like—and you come along, stir things up again," said Tork.

"Don't worry," said Aggie.

"We're a dying breed," snapped Tork.

"I know."

"And you come along and give them false hope."

"You never know, with the shed and the Petri dishes," muttered Aggie.

Tork threw her a look.

"The Washerwoman will have you strung up like a G-string if she knew. She'd give anything for a child."

Aggie looked at her pal with her best reassuring face. "It will all fall into place, just you wait and see. Nothing can go wrong in that shed of yours."

Chapter Thirty-Two

THE LIBRARIAN'S LAST STAND

"The hemp tea on an empty stomach had women babbling like a baby or laughing like one."–The Washerwoman

*L*M-2 was never quite sure what her brains were for until she stared out of her window at the dwindling four-legged creatures.

She saw the need to save things, create a haven for the four-legged creatures, and she had ideas about the sun, wind, and water, cleaner ways to run a city. But would anyone listen?

Only James the Strong listened, but he didn't have clue. He, hypnotized by LM-2's mouth, quietly stared as she talked; she was so like Aggie it astounded him. In fact, he often told LM-2 how much like Aggie she was, which really pissed her off—especially when, mid bed-diving, he moaned, "Aggie used to do this . . . but for much longer."

LM-2 stared into the night; Aggie was back. This so-called master in the bedroom who made *her* life hell had left her own son—a mere eleven-year-old boy.

Well, thought LM-2, *she'll not last for long. Not if I have anything to do with things.*

❖

The Librarian was an excellent spy. He loitered about the market, the Institute, and the traders in his "demented old git" disguise, picking up many scams. He was so good at incognito listening that he, catching tax dodgers, saved enough money to waste on the building of a statue for his leader. A statue that had him not only in the leader's favor but "right up his royal arse," as Reader Two so eloquently put it.

And he was prepared to do more.

He just needed to know what that "more" was, and when he, dressed as a deaf old woman and aimlessly passing a trading post, heard talks of a needle raid, the "more" jumped out at him like a snake in the grass . . .

He pulled out his favorite "melodrama villain" cloak from the closet and wrapped it around himself.

I'll rid this city of that damnable Aggie, he thought, *and the books, the extra-large mirrors, and the esteemed Leader will be mine—forever.*

He let out a villainous laugh, then, catching sight of his reflection, realized that he looked quite mad and stopped.

Chapter Thirty-Three

THE POSSE

"There is more to a four-legged creature than a name."—Cat

*T*he Aliens crept into the silent city, winding their way around parked transporters. They stopped at the main street and stared up at the sky-high buildings silhouetted by the bright light of the Milky Way.

In the distance were the makings of a courtyard. Arthur of the North's statue stood in the middle, floodlit in yellow light with a sea of flowers at the feet. Beside it were the makings of James the Strong's statue—a pair of enormous feet—and leaning against the feet waiting for erecting were two gates with "The Courtyard of Greatness" engraved across the top.

The Aliens stared at the large toenail curled towards the sky. Statues were as necessary as a hairnet to an Alien and the flower-laying as ridiculous as one.

"You could park a spaceship on that toe," muttered Maisie.

"Quiet," hushed Tork.

"I mean how big can a man be?" said Maisie.

"Pretty big," muttered Aggie.

"Ridiculous," muttered Cat. "Days of work for what? A toe uglier than a nose-picking. Three men it took"—she turned to Aggie—"for one toe."

"What?" said Aggie with a "how do you know?" look.

"You think we've never been here before?" said Maisie.

"Well, yes," said Aggie. "There is a security system."

"The one we just walked past?" said the Washerwoman.

"Keep it down," whispered Tork.

A rat scurried past, its mechanical tail flopping at the Bin Emptier's feet. She picked it up and waved at her comrades.

"Told you . . . humungous."

Aggie looked at her. "You've been here too?"

"Will you tone it down," hissed Tork.

"And here's me making maps and drawing diagrams," muttered Aggie.

"This place is an eco–time bomb," muttered the Bin Emptier.

"*Shhhh*," said Tork.

"'*Shhhh*'? This place is deader than my ovaries," said the Washerwoman.

The Librarian, like a bat, slid from his room, crept down the corridor, and slipped out into the night, and with a sideward glance that would incriminate a nun, he made for his ruse: the leader's transporter, parked with prime viewing, the smoky glass making excellent "I can see you but you can't see me" viewing.

He clicked open the door and slid in.

"Did you hear that?" said Tork.

"What?" hissed the Washerwoman.

"Just a rat," muttered Cat. "They don't exactly tiptoe."

"Sounded like a window opening," muttered Aggie.

Tork turned on her. "Could you say that any louder?"

Aggie, Tork, and Cat watched as Maisie, the Washerwoman, and the Bin Emptier cut through the courtyard toward the Institute. Maisie knew the place "like the back of my hand"; the Washerwoman, being the shed expert, knew what was needed and had a pretty good understanding of a Petri dish, and the Bin Emptier was an expert wall climber.

Aggie jumped. "I'm sure I heard a window shut." She looked about. "Or was it a transporter?"

"Shout louder," snapped Tork. "I don't think they heard you at the Art Centre."

Fanny, from her husband's penthouse office, gazed down at the Aliens. She, wondering what on earth they were doing, cursed herself for allowing this LM-2 upstart to take over.

She believed all women were not only equal but essentially good and found it hard to swallow LM-2's rage against a fellow "sister."

The others swallowed LM-2's rage whole and were prepared to do anything to stop that "slapper" from whatever she had planned. Some even claimed that she was "in cahoots with the leader."

If only we had weapons, thought Fanny, *we could storm like real troopers, take over . . . I know that Aggie would follow.*

She sighed. Her posse was due any minute, and they had as much idea of storming as she did Aggie's plans and as much idea of espionage as she did "knocking up a soufflé."

They knocked at the door. She jumped and, without shifting her gaze, yelled, "It's open."

The Poet and the Warden barged in, stopping as soon as they entered. The foyer was larger than their street.

"Great pickling sperm, you could hide a spaceship in here," snapped the warden.

Fanny, with a "keep it down" look at the Warden, silently shut her window.

"They're heading for the library," said the Poet.

"And the Institute," said the Beverage Maker.

Fanny stopped. "The Institute?"

The women nodded.

"Probably after needles," muttered the Poet. "A Petri dish is not worth a soya bean without one."

Fanny, with a "never thought of that" look, turned to the Beverage Maker. "We need to split up."

"We've already split up; LM-2 and the others are heading for the library. We're to head across the courtyard."

"I knew that," lied Fanny.

Aggie, Tork, and Cat made their way to the library. The entrance was a grand affair.

The Foreigners, mimicking a Victorian department store, had erected a fancy canopy over the facade of windows to hide the statue of Wife-ie's Hubby. Behind the windows were scenes of stuffed four-legged creatures clutching books in an animated fashion. The city dwellers found it funny. The Aliens and Foreigners, however, averted their eyes with respect, apart from Cat, who, with a dramatic shake of her fist, hissed a venomous "Bastards."

None saw the Librarian peering from his transporter. They were too busy arguing over which entrance to use. Cat wanted to swing through a window "like a tree-dwelling creature," using "that pickling waste of statue" as her starting point.

Tork suggested the back door.

"I brought extra rope," said Cat as they headed around the back, "and swinging is way more spy-like."

"It's an in-and-out job," hissed Tork. "The stairs are quicker."

"Pfff, stairs," muttered Cat. "Old ladies use stairs."

Aggie, like she had done a million times before, pressed the combination on the lock. When that didn't work, Tork, with a "see," pulled out a tool and eased the door ajar.

Aggie, with a pinched face, made to push her way in.

Tork stopped her.

"We need to disengage the alarm first," she said.

"I knew that," lied Aggie.

Maisie, the Bin Emptier, and the Washerwoman raced like army cadets across the courtyard, unaware that Fanny and her posse were approaching.

Hearing marching noises, they jumped behind the big toe of James the Strong's statue.

"Shit," hissed Maisie.

"Shhhh," snapped the Washerwoman.

A massive mechanical turtle marched by, dwarfing James the Strong's foot.

"It's only a turtle," muttered Bin Emptier.

The other two looked at her. "Turtle?"

"Do you not watch the mirrors when you come here?" said the Bin Emptier. "That thing is a pure copy, nothing to worry about."

"Nothing to worry about? It could squash us with its big toe."

"Turtles[1] merely lay eggs," said the Bin Emptier.

"Well, I ain't gonna be near that thing when it lays," said the Washerwoman.

The turtle stopped, blinked, looked about, let a long wheezing noise from its behind, then carried on.

"Follow that turtle," hissed Maisie, who liked to think she was in charge.

The Washerwoman glared at her.

"At a distance," muttered Maisie.

The library was dark, filled with only the low hum of men snoring.

The Librarian watched Aggie, Tork, and Cat slip into the library.

He grinned. *Predictable,* he thought, so *perfectly* predictable.

He was about to move . . . when he saw LM-2 flash like a ninja across the street.

Holy sperm.

The Sidekick followed inches from him.

Holy mother of sperm.

The Beverage Maker, lagging behind, skidded past the transporter and tripped.

The Librarian jolted, triggering the transporter alarm.

The Beverage Maker stopped like she had been electrocuted.

The Librarian froze.

"Kick it," hissed the Sidekick.

"What?" said the Beverage Maker.

"Kick!" said the Sidekick, landing her foot into the side of the transporter.

The transporter lit up like a Christmas tree, setting off the next transporter. Siren noises echoed down the street.

Window lights flicked on.

"Bollocks," hissed all three as LM-2 appeared from the corner, mouthing "idiots" with a variety of gestures.

Tork froze; Aggie halted; Cat, like a bat, pressed herself against the wall.

They waited as the sirens reverberated through the library.

"We're being spied upon," said Cat.

---

1. *The great innovation of those in the art centre, when they grew tired of transporting things, little did they know where it would lead.*

Chapter Thirty-Four

CAMOUFLAGE

"Never ignore a charging turtle."–Fanny

The turtle, puffing and belching, made her way to the Institute as Maisie's posse, charging from one hiding place to the next, followed.

The turtle stopped at the Institute and waited.

Maisie's posse skidded behind a transporter and watched.

A large, camouflaged garage door lifted open.

The turtle marched into the darkness.

Quickly, Maisie gestured.

They scurried behind the turtle as the door began to close.

Maisie threw herself under the door; the Bin Emptier followed.

The Washerwoman, at the rear, tripped . . .

Maisie, with a "you can do it" look, stretched out her hand.

The Washerwoman, throwing herself into a superb footballer's skid, slid under the door inches from closing . . .

The door juddered to a halt just shy of her backside.

She rolled into the shadows.

Maisie and the Bin Emptier let out a hissed cheer and almost applauded until they heard footsteps approaching . . .

Their eyes adjusted to the shadows; the turtle filled the space, and the footsteps were coming from behind on both sides.

"Bollocks," echoed a male voice from the right.

The Washerwoman stopped, the Bin Emptier froze, as Maisie, quicker than a lizard's tongue, pinned both against the wall with a "don't even breathe" hiss.

The footsteps clipped nearer.

The women held their breath.

"Damnable remote," said the male voice from the right.

Maisie caught a flash from his torch, grabbed her two comrades, and rolled under the turtle.

Flat on their backs, they stared at the turtle's belly heaving up and down inches from their nose. The turtle's stomach rumbled, it belched; the women held their breath, Maisie silently gagging.

"That remote is as much use as a spaceship," said the male from the right. "And as for that frigging door—"

He kicked it.

"Very scientific," muttered a male from the left.

The Washerwoman pointed to the feet of the two males by the door.

"They've all the money in the world for pickling statues, but will they give us a decent remote, proper batteries, a door that shuts? I mean how are we to develop wasp-eaters when there's not even money for remote batteries?"

"We're supposed to use our initiative," muttered the male from the left.

"Initiative don't pay for batteries. Why don't they use their initiative and make statues out of that hot air of theirs?"

"Shhhh," hissed the male from the left. "Walls have ears."

"You mean that slimy Librarian? This is what I think of him," snapped the male from the right.

The remote ricocheted across the room, bouncing off the wall and hitting the door.

The door burst into action, opening again.

The turtle jolted, looked over its shoulder, then began to shuffle a turn.

"Not again," muttered the male from the left.

The women scrabbled underneath as the turtle began a tanklike about-face.

"It's like it's trying to escape," muttered the male from the left. "You'd think it was alive. You'd better stop it."

"You stop it."

"You hurled the remote," snapped the male from the left.

The turtle, mid three-point turn, knocked over the voice from the right.

"We can't let it leave again," muttered the voice from the left. "They'll go mad."

The male from the right jumped to his feet. "Well, if we had a decent door, this wouldn't be a problem."

The turtle grunted, picking up speed.

The door was now wide open.

"Quick," said the voice from the left. "You can grab its tail from your side."

"OK, keep your spacesuit on."

"I said *quick*, smart-arse, they'll be here any minute," said the voice from the left.

"Who cares," said the voice from the right with a halfhearted grab.

"Just grab the door then."

"What, with my six-foot arms?" said the voice from the right.

"Just jump, will you?" snapped the voice from the left.

"And then what?"

"Oh, for pickle's sake, *pull*," snapped the voice from the left.

The turtle, now facing the open door, burst into a trot.

The women scrabbled for something to hang on to.

They could hear more footsteps approaching, distant shouting and cursing.

"Great spouting sperm," boomed a voice over the others, sending the turtle into a speed befitting a fire.

The women had seconds . . .

Maisie, thinking on her back, gestured to the opening at the turtle's backside, and before either could pull a face, she grabbed the two women, slid, rolled, and jumped into the backside of the turtle as it charged through the opening.

With a thump, they landed in darkness, engulfed in the rhythmic pulsing of the turtle's heart and lungs.

The Washerwoman huffed as they tried to stand.

"Now what do we do?" she shouted into Maisie's ear.

"Feel our way," yelled Maisie with a stumble.

The Washerwoman crashed against her.

"Not me!" snapped Maisie.

The Bin Emptier, still on her back, fumbled for her flashlight and flicked it on with a grunt.

They look around and gasped at what they saw.

Fanny ran, dived, summersaulted, and hid across the courtyard like a stuntwoman in a movie.

The Warden and the Poet walked, stopping at the feet of James the Strong's statue.

Fanny scanned the horizon as the Warden and the Poet discussed the budget for such a big toe and matching family member.

Fanny stared into the distance. *Is that a turtle?*

The Warden and the Poet, now standing on the big toe, ignored her.

"It's marching," whispered Fanny.

"They always do that when they escape," said the Warden, holding her hand against the toenail for scale.

"Pointless," muttered the Poet, comparing hands.

Fanny looked at her.

"I mean what's the point of a robot if you can't control it?" muttered the Poet.

At first, Maisie and her posse didn't say a thing; they were too busy trying to stay standing inside a turtle sprinting on uneven ground.

Maisie grabbed onto something slimy, let go, touched her face, realized what she had done, and gagged.

There was a complex network of greased tubes that would give a plumber nightmares, enough wiring to electrocute an army of elephants, and a pulsating fuse box the size of a transporter, beside which, humming with activity, sat a compact minibar—some would say a fridge.

"Who needs a minibar inside a turtle?" said the Bin Emptier.

"You sure it's not a fridge?" said Maisie.

"It looks like a fridge," said the Washerwoman.

She staggered to the minibar and stared through the glass door. "It's full of eggs," she said.

"Don't touch the minibar," said the Bin Emptier.

"Mountains of them," muttered the Washerwoman. She smiled at the two women. "And Petri dishes . . ." She looked again. "I think I saw a needle too."

"Perhaps you should leave it," said Maisie.

The Washerwoman looked closer at *a row of test tubes.*

Her heart began to thump. *Could it be . . . ?*

The turtle jolted.

She steadied herself using its inner wall.

The turtle belched.

She peered closer, fogging up the glass. *Test tubes of seeds—glorious seeds!*

She turned to her colleagues. "Seeds," she shouted just as the turtle tripped, tossing the women about like a dinghy at high tide.

The Washerwoman righted herself on the minibar.

She made to wipe the glass.

"Just leave it," hissed the Bin Emptier.

"Probably best," said Maisie.

The Washerwoman stopped. "Leave it?" She looked at them. "There are *seeds* in there. The last thing I'm gonna do is *leave* it."

She reached for the door.

"Don't touch!" yelled the Bin Emptier.

The washer pulled at the handle.

"Shit," muttered Maisie.

Fanny stared at the turtle; it was approaching way too fast for a turtle. An uneasy sense of foreboding hit her . . .

"It looks different somehow, like it knows what it's doing," she said.

"It was in my garden the other week—right mess of the tulips," muttered the Poet. "Had to use daisies for my statues."

"Pfff, daisies—they last all of an afternoon," said the Warden.

"It's heading here," said Fanny.

"What?"

"I think it's running," said Fanny.

"Running? A turtle? I hardly think so," muttered the Warden.

She stopped.

The turtle was getting closer by the minute.

"Shit," said the Warden.

Fanny, pulling a whip from her tool belt and letting out an "I've got this" yell, unleashed her whip into the air.

Her comrades, having no idea about whips, stared as the whip wrapped around the Arthur of the North statue's arm of glory thrust into the air and clutching a recycle bin bag.

Fanny, like Spiderman, sailed through the air, landing on the pinnacle of Wifi-ie's obelisk and overshadowing the turtle. She jumped, landing on its back.

The turtle squawked like a crow and collapsed on its belly.

Chapter Thirty-Five

THE RAID

"Tiptoeing is not something Aliens were good at; neither was whispering."–Aggie

*L*M-2 slid under the transporter and silenced it, and before the others had time to cheer, she appeared, dusted herself down, and gestured for the women to follow.

The Librarian, itching to get his hands on those damnable women, watched as they headed for the back entrance of the library. He snuck from the transporter, tripped, hissed a "bollocks," and righted himself.

"What was that?" said LM-2, poised at the door as the Librarian, like a vampire, disappeared up the wall—straight for the window of Aggie's old room.

Aggie headed up the stairs behind Tork as Cat waited by the stairs. She knew they were being followed the moment the transporter siren blasted into action, and damned if she was going to miss the opportunity of a good fight.

She saw the cloaked git who had set it off. . . .

There was something familiar about him, the way he slid from behind the transporter . . .

She waited by the window, caught a glimpse of the Librarian scaling the wall, and realized where she had seen that slide before: from her trading days, when secrets got out quicker than a hill fire.

Nothing better, she thought, *than a fight on a window ledge with an old git who can't keep his mouth shut.*

❖

Aggie and Tork headed for Aggie's old room. The door was locked, the corridor was quiet; she jiggled the handle, inspected the combination, and swore, her cheeks hot with anger.

She'd hardly been gone a week.

"They've changed the locks," she huffed.

"What do you expect?" said Tork.

"But that's my room."

"Not anymore," muttered Tork.

"I mean what am I, a criminal?"

"You've been ousted, tossed aside," said Tork.

Aggie threw Tork a look.

"Given the flick like a burnt-out transporter," said Tork.

"The things I've done for this town—for that man," Aggie huffed. "One sniff of a younger model and I'm out quicker than a bird drops it's load."

"That's bed-diving for you," said Tork.

Aggie tutted.

"Genitals have no loyalty," said Tork.

"Cheers."

"One sniff," said Tork, "and they rise like bread in the oven."

"OK, I get the picture," snapped Aggie.

She stopped; two rats scurried past, followed by the pushing of a broom across the polished floor.

Tork slid behind a bin, Aggie the water cooler.

A pissed-off-looking middle-aged cleaner appeared. Aggie watched as she tossed a paper cup into a corner bin.

"All's quiet," she shouted over her shoulder.

"Apart from you," shouted a female voice from down the corridor.

"Told you that Librarian lives in fantasyland—there's no one here."

"Past it," yelled the voice. "Been on the herbals for too long. Should be put out to graze with the four-legged creatures."

Aggie and Tork watched as a younger, brighter-looking cleaner joined the first.

"Serves him right," said the older cleaner, "spreading rumors, setting those women up. I mean I'm no Aggie fan—"

Tork threw Aggie a soft look.

"—but she didn't deserve the lies he told LM-2."

Aggie stopped. *Lies?*

"Stroke of genius," said the younger cleaner.

The older woman threw her a "pardon?" look.

"If they got together, James the Strong wouldn't stand a chance." She pulled a cup from the dispenser and filled it.

The older cleaner nodded. "That's true."

The second cleaner downed her water with an "arrrrh . . . could have make some changes in this hole of a place."

She tossed her cup at the bin with perfect aim. "Pity, I liked her."

"Too big for her boots," muttered the older woman.

"What do you expect? She's a slapper," said the younger woman. "Takes guts to slap."

"Well, strictly speaking, it wasn't her . . ." said the older woman.

"Oh, forgot about that." She laughed. "My ol' man says they should have palmed her off on some ol' git, someone who's way past all that bed-diving."

The older cleaner arched her back with a groan. "What I wouldn't give for one of those."

They laughed, heading down the corridor.

"Men," said the younger cleaner. "You can't live with 'em and you can't live without 'em."

Aggie, with a fierce look, slid from the water cooler, pulled a tool from Tork's belt, and, just as Tork had earlier, budged her door open.

❖

LM-2, with visions of putting Aggie in her place and more, headed upstairs with a "follow me" to her posse.

The Sidekick and the Beverage Maker, with no such vision, crept behind. Neither noticed the bat-like Librarian pass a window . . .

The Librarian had scaled the building like a lizard up a tree. His limber body was a superb tool for spying: he could climb mountains, trapeze across a circus tent, and tiptoe like a ballerina on a windowsill the width of a pencil. He, like Cat, had no fear of heights but, unlike her, had an aversion to fighting; he preferred a "surprise and push" maneuver, preferably off somewhere high.

Within minutes, he had passed windows, drainpipes, and the odd dripping rowan to land like a caped crusader outside Aggie's old room. As the midnight air fluttered across his cheeks, his thin chest gasped with excitement.

So close . . .

Aggie's window was in the corner of the building, a perching haven for mechanical birds. Oblivious to the large bird letting go of an equally large portion of barbecued flesh, the Librarian, poised by the window, smiled at the idea of sliding in and pushing. *Hopefully Aggie.*

He had no idea of Cat behind the window next door, nor her expert whip-wielding.

He skidded on the bird dropping, righted himself, and, with a "bollocking pickle," rubbed his leg . . . until he caught sight of Cat's leg sliding from the next window.

He stopped.

Another leg followed, along with Cat's wrinkled face.

He laughed.

She was as old as a spaceship.

Her hand went for her whip.

The Librarian looked about, quickly realizing he was hemmed in.

Cat pulled out her whip.

The Librarian made for the window; it was locked.

Shit.

Cat took aim.

The Librarian attempted a "breaking glass with elbow" move, forgetting the glass was as thick as James the Strong.

He rubbed his elbow. *Shit.*

Cat, with a superb fly-fishing cast, flicked her whip; it licked around the Librarian's ankle and took hold.

"Great pickling walnut," he shouted, his voice echoing down the corridors.

The two cleaners heading for the cleaner's cupboard didn't even stop. "Told you, crazy." Said the middle age cleaner.

"Complete fruit loop," muttered the younger cleaner."

Aggie heard the Librarian's scream while piling her boxes into Tork's backpack.

"That'll be Cat," muttered Tork. "She mentioned something about a spy."

Aggie stopped. Behind Tork stood LM-2 in the doorway like a superhero prepared to defend her city.

In the courtyard, mechanical birds circled the turtle menacingly as Fanny, astride it, tried to maintain her balance.

Maisie took charge.

Hurled from the anus of the turtle as it fell, she jumped to her feet, caught sight of Fanny's whip, grabbed the end of it, and pulled herself onto the turtle's back.

That turtle was going nowhere without her . . .

Fanny watched the Alien scale the turtle like an expert mountaineer, not slipping even as the turtle tried to shuffle its feet.

As Maisie reached the top, the turtle let out a cough, spewing the Bin Emptier and the Washerwoman from her backside. Fanny faltered, Maisie caught her, and their eyes met.

Fanny skidded, stumbled, and almost fell off the humped back until

Maisie, clutching the whip with one hand, grabbed Fanny with the other and pulled.

Again, their eyes met, and for a moment, they forgot they were balancing on a turtle's back.

Chapter Thirty-Six

A POUNCE TOO FAR

"The Aliens heard many things about the Foreigners, and the Foreigners thought they knew all about the Aliens. Truth was, they came from the same place and forgot."—Cat

"Who are you?" said the Warden.

"Who are *you*?" said the Bin Emptier.

"I asked first," said the Warden.

"So?" snapped the Bin Emptier. She stopped; the face was familiar. They eyed each other.

"Didn't we trade?" said the Bin Emptier.

The Warden's face lit up; the Bin Emptier had given her a good deal. "I remember" was on the tip of her tongue when the turtle began to huff and snort as it tried to rise to its feet.

It staggered and stumbled.

Fanny skidded; Maisie grabbed her.

"Too big for her legs," muttered the Washerwoman. "Design fault."

"I heard that too." The Poet nodded.

The turtle blinked and collapsed.

A mechanical bird circled closer, spotted Maisie's bobbing red hair, and made a dive.

Fanny pulled a raisin from her pocket and tossed it at the bird with a "there you go, honey."

"Honey?" Maisie flashed a look.

"Design fault," muttered the Washerwoman. "Red sets 'em off—stops them picking at crops but not great in cities."

Fanny laughed; she had pockets full of raisins. She tossed more into the distance and the birds flew off. The turtle looked over it's shoulder and licked it's lips.

"You want one too?" said Fanny.

The turtle blinked with a nod.

Fanny tossed a few into its mouth and turned to Maisie. "It's like it's alive."

"I think it's a she," said Maisie.

For a moment, the turtle seemed to relax, chew with pleasure.

Fanny scratched the top of it's head.

The turtle purred.

"Another design fault," muttered the Poet. "Sensory implants—designed for control, but they make the robotic more . . . well, bribable."

The Washerwoman nodded with an "I heard that too."

"They'll be breeding next," muttered Maisie.

LM-2 eyed Aggie, the so-called mother who had left her son.

"That boy is crying his eyes out because of you," she said. "You should be ashamed of yourself."

Tork, mid backpacking, stopped. "You've got the wrong end of things," she said.

The two women posed for a silent "you're a cow" stare.

The Librarian flashed past the window with a scream.

LM-2 stopped. "The Librarian?"

He screamed again.

They ran to the window to see the Librarian wrestling with a whip and Cat in a ninja stance gleefully tugging.

He pulled his leg free with a grunt.

"*That's* the Librarian?" said Tork.

Aggie and LM-2 nodded as Cat pounced like a miniature Bruce Lee.

She was an impressive sight. So impressive that no one heard the Beverage Maker and the Sidekick appear, or the two cleaners.

Watching a fight on a window ledge can do that to a person, especially when the fighters were old enough to know better . . . .

The two posses joined forces to help the turtle up onto her legs. They head-patted, cooed, lifted, and, finally, with a uniformed push, cheered as the turtle stood.

Fanny threw a few more raisins into the turtle's mouth as the women continued to pat.

"We could design something better," said the Washerwoman, "around the legs here. I mean, take this back leg here."

The turtle attempted to lift her leg; the Washerwoman helped.

The others nodded.

"Perhaps a pulley system?" muttered the Poet.

"Pulley system," laughed the Washerwoman. "In your dreams. It's levers you want."

"Maybe some cords," muttered Maisie, "with perhaps a concertina-like action here?"

Fanny stroked her back as the women talked, discussed, and occasionally prodded.

The turtle basked in the attention, and when the Washerwoman suggested the best place to do all this reconstruction was back at her shed "where no Settler could interfere," the turtle lifted her eyes to the sky with a high-pitched crow.

❖

The Librarian, gaining control and with a tussle that surprised even him, grabbed the whip and pinned Cat to the wall.

Aggie gasped. "Should we help?"

"Nah, she's just toying with him," muttered Tork.

Cat began to make choking noises.

"You sure?" said LM-2.

"She always does that," said Tork.

"Help me," croaked Cat.

Aggie threw a look at Tork.

"Just acting," muttered Tork.

"Her lips are blue," said LM-2.

"Drama queen can't help herself," said Tork.

"I'm going down . . ." cried Cat feebly.

The Librarian thrust his head back with his best diabolical laugh. "Ha, ha, ha . . ."

Aggie jumped to help.

LM-2 made to join her.

Tork pulled them back as Cat shoved her hand into a place the Librarian least expected.

A place no one had seen for years . . . a place that was as out of date as the has-been spaceship and had seen just as little action.

Cat rummaged. Where was "it"?

"She'll be ages trying to find anything down there," muttered the older cleaner.

"Perhaps we should help?" said the Sidekick. "They *are* kind of old."

"Nah," said the older cleaner. "Look at him—he's confused. He probably hasn't touched it in years."

Fanny led the turtle as the two posses headed into the main street.

Fanny talked of networking, joining forces, and suffragettes.

The Poet and the Bin Emptier talked of trading while the Wanden and the Washerwoman pontificated over pulley systems, until the Washerwoman mentioned her shed.

"Hmm, heard of those," muttered the Poet.

"Shelving like you've never seen," muttered the Bin Emptier.

"Perfect for a fridge," said the Washerwoman.

The turtle stopped.

"It's a minibar," said the Warden. "And that turtle will never let you take hers."

They stared at each other.

"A new dawn has risen." Fanny eyed the two women. "The age of women."

"A minibar," said the Washerwoman, "is for drinks. What I saw was a fridge, and that *fridge* is perfect for our shed."

"Never come between a turtle and her minibar," said the Poet. "They are the guardians, very possessive—only men in white coats can get near."

The turtle shook her head.

"All we need is weapons . . . underwire," muttered Fanny.

"Even the dullest of turtles will go crazy," said the Warden.

The turtle glared at the Warden.

"And it's not yours to take."

"Who says?" snapped the Washerwoman.

The Washerwoman thought of all those years yearning for a baby as her ovaries turned to dust, her partner's once-majestic family member shrunk to a pea.

The longing had never gone away . . .

She glared at the Warden. "What we need is in that fridge," said the Washerwoman, "and if it weren't for us having to make your super-deluxe, maximum-efficiency soya, we wouldn't need that pickle-ridden thing."

"A design fault," muttered the Poet, "in the soya. You can't bugger about with hormones and get away with it."

"Oh, I see—it's all my fault, is it?" snapped the Warden.

Lights flicked on in a few windows.

"That fridge is mine," shouted the Washerwoman. "And those seeds in that fridge are mine, and there's nothing you or anyone can do to stop me—"

"Keep the noise down," shouted a voice from a window. "Some of us are trying to get some sleep."

"Oh, we'll see about that!" hissed the Warden.

The Washerwoman pushed the Warden; the Warden pushed back.

"Ladies, please—not in front of the turtle," hissed Fanny.

A cry came from above.

The turtle, with a snort, gestured to Aggie's old room.

The two posses looked up to see Cat and the Librarian on a window ledge like something out of *Mission Impossible*.

The Librarian clutched his groin, let out a high-pitched yelp, and stumbled away.

A few more lights flicked on in the street.

Cat pounced—lethal on a ledge full of bird droppings—and the Librarian hurtled to the ground.

"Nooooo . . ." echoed through the main street.

Lights flicked on everywhere as mechanical birds perched on lamp-posts screeched and fluttered like a flock of crows.

The Librarian plummeted, crashing onto the canopy.

"What was that?" shouted a voice from a window.

"Don't know," shouted another.

He bounced, flopped, and groaned, his right leg slung over the side of the turtle like a string of overcooked spaghetti.

There was a tear; a high heel appeared, followed by a loud rip, a pointed shoe, and then a stockinged left leg.

Fanny jumped onto the turtle and peered at the Librarian. She shook him.

He screamed in pain.

"He's alive," shouted Fanny.

"Tough man," muttered the older cleaner.

"That he is," muttered the younger cleaner.

"Poor fella. Feel sorry for him," muttered the Sidekick.

"*Poor fella*," said the older cleaner. "You wouldn't be saying that if you knew the poison he spread."

"And he tried to kill me," said Cat, climbing in from the window.

"He's a liar, a muck-spreader," said the younger cleaner.

They stared down at the elegantly dressed crumbled figure.

"Such a small man too," said Tork.

The canopy ripped, tore, and burst open.

The Librarian tumbled onto the steps below. His glazed eyes stared straight up into the turtle's.

"I'm done for," he croaked and passed out.

Chapter Thirty-Seven

TARZAN

"There is more to a turtle than a shell."–Fanny

*J*ames the Strong woke from his sleep, in the middle of a nightmare with *that damnable Librarian screaming...*
He rolled over, stretched out for his princess, and found a pillow.

He sat up, switched the light on, and rubbed his face.

"Princess? Buttercup?"

He looked about. Was she in the john?

Then he heard a faint "he's alive," followed by more yelling.

He jumped and, with a "who was that" look, raced through his living quarters into the room with a view of the main street.

He stared into the night.

The windows were lit up, and folk were staring out their windows.

He looked down to see the back of a giant turtle . . . which from the height of his room was more like a pincushion.

"Princess?" he yelled.

His voice echoed down the street.

"Princess!!" he shouted.

The crowd stopped; the turtle looked up.

More window lights flicked on.

LM-2 stopped.

Aggie caught her eye.

"Shit."

"Is that who I think it is?" said Tork.

The two women nodded.

LM-2 began to peel her clothes off, revealing nightclothes underneath.

"You'd better go," she said, shoving her "spying" clothes into a cupboard. "He'll be flying down that corridor any minute."

"He moves like the wind when confused," muttered Aggie.

LM-2 nodded. "And fobbing him off will take ages."

"Longer than finding a family member on that Librarian," muttered Aggie.

She caught LM-2's eye—a smile flickered across their faces.

"We've got mops," said the older cleaner. "We can head him off at the pass, buy you some time."

"Excellent," said LM-2 as Tork, grabbing their backpacks, headed for the window . . .

Aggie followed.

The cleaners, with exaggerated laughs, clattered out the door; with voices as loud as foghorns, they began their banter.

"Some fall, that."

"That's what comes from too much hemp."

"Aye, too much hemp will do it."

LM-2 followed. She stopped at the door and turned to the Beverage Maker and the Sidekick.

"Don't move till you hear me moaning," she said and, with a "comrade" gesture of solidarity, headed out the door.

The Sidekick and Beverage Maker watched with admiration. Never had they seen such dedication.

Cat looked out on a sea of lit-up windows and pulled out her rope; she had waited her whole life for such a moment.

Quickly making a lasso, she turned to Tork and Aggie "we have as much time as a sneeze."

She tossed her lasso. "You go first."

Tork wrapped her arms around Aggie's waist and looked into her eyes.

"Trust me," she said, pulling Aggie tighter, and before Aggie could nod a "yes," Tork jumped, sailing through the air like Tarzan.

Aggie, pinned to Tork, gasped as the wind whistled through her hair. Tork's grip was so tight they felt like one.

Cat followed, grabbing the return rope; with a wink at the Sidekick and the Beverage Maker, she jumped, disappearing into the night like Spiderman.

The Sidekick and Beverage Maker leaned out the window, watching as the three women landed with a soft plop on the turtle and rode away—minutes before the crowds arrived.

"History in the making," muttered the Sidekick.

The Beverage Maker nodded. "If only the Poet was here."

It didn't take long for the two males who had allowed the turtle to escape to appear. Jack and John charged into the street and arrived to find a crowd muttering about a "has-been addict, completely out of it."

They pushed through to find the Librarian sprawled out on the steps, his legs as twisted as an arthritic ninety-year-old, rambling about a "whip-wielding ninja" and a "giant turtle with the breath of a drainpipe."

"Past it," yelled a driver. "The man should be put out to graze with the four-legged creatures."

"His grazing days are over," muttered another.

"Turtle?" said Jack. "How big?"

Chapter Thirty-Eight

ABDUCTION

"If only you men listened to us women."—Wife-ie "If only you women communicated."—Arthur of the North

Over the next few nights, Aggie and the Aliens slid in and out of the city on the back of the turtle pilfering like children in a sweetshop. LM-2, Fanny, and her posse more than helped: they planned, plotted, and made diagrams during their late-night spaceship meetings. Not that the Aliens took much notice, but they were smart enough to know not to bite the hand that had "inside info," let alone talked of "weapons of mass destruction."

Soon the shed was bulging with test tubes, Petri dishes, and enough eggs and seeds to recreate an army, and Cat had the makings of a library, despite the fact that the other Aliens had as much interest in a library as in flower arranging.

Jack and John followed the trail of the turtle, to a trading post where the trail had "gone cold." Standing by the roadside examining the end of trail of raisins and massive footprints, they scratched their heads.

"Why do the footprints just stop?" muttered John mid shrub-rummaging. He looked up. "Did she explode?"

"Who knows?" said Jack, who shrugged and was just on the verge of suggesting a possible "story for the boss" when all went dark, thanks to a hemp bag over their heads.

Jack and John put up a fight of muffled swearing and shoving until the inhaling of hemp scent knocked them for six.

Captured, drugged, their seed extracted like the juicing of a lemon, they lay stupefied in a hut, and the Aliens were at a loss of what to do next . . .

LM-2, after leaving a comatose James the Strong to snore, headed into the night to the "what to pilfer next" meeting held in the spaceship.

The spaceship, thanks to the Librarian being "out of action," was overflowing with cleaners, many cluttered about the beverage-making station and annoying the Beverage Maker with pleas of "can I have a go?"

LM-2 came across Aggie and Fanny arguing over the fate of the two men.

There was talk of memory-erasing, and Fanny, who was into human rights regardless of genitals, felt the removal of memories was on par with slicing up four-legged creatures' flesh.

"If they remember anything, the Aliens are done for," said Aggie.

LM-2 eyed Aggie.

"Those two men," said Aggie, "will tell James the Strong every-thing, and what do you think he will do?"

"Build a statue?" muttered Fanny, attempting a witty look.

A cleaner, mid caffeine-pilfering, laughed.

"He'll tell the Librarian," said Aggie.

LM-2 nodded. Aggie, surprisingly, made sense.

"He tells him every pickling thing," said Aggie. "Then who knows what will happen to the suffragettes?"

Fanny turned to LM-2 with a "what do you think?" look.

She blushed, not really wanting to agree with her rival in public.

Aggie and LM-2 avoided each other at all costs. It was not easy to forget the past, despite having more things in common than not (saving the planet and keeping Fanny and her "weapons of mass destruction" dreams in line being but two).

"We need to cover our tracks," LM-2 muttered. "Hemp is the only way."

Aggie threw her a "you agree with me" look.

"It'll bugger up their memory," said LM-2. "Give us time."

Fanny looked at the women.

"When did you two get so cozy?"

Aggie and LM-2 shifted uncomfortably; they hadn't realized they had.

The room was silent . . .

"Those two?" blurted a young cleaner. "They are as thick as my man's family member, and that's not something you want to clap eyes on when you're looking for a good night's sleep."

Aggie and LM-2 laughed so loudly they were told to stop.

Then Fanny, finally convinced by Aggie's "the joys of hemp," argument, gave in, ordering the cleaners to leave the caffeine to the Beverage Maker and do what they did best: "Clean up."

A week later, James and John, clutching painful groins, were found at the entrance of the Institute by two cleaners "on their way to the market."

Dazed and stupefied, mumbling incoherently about terrible knock-knock jokes and a dancing turtle, they were deemed addicts of an unknown substance and taken into the Institute for healing, only to surface for the odd spaceship-pulling day.

The Librarian spent six months in the Institute learning how to get about with legs as useful as a second nose and as mobile. Those in the Institute experimented with needles, trying to rejuvenate the Librarian's legs, but in the end, all they could come up with was a motorized wheelchair.

Never again did he snigger like Mutley the cartoon dog or laugh like a demonic maniac. Smiling was something he gave up the minute he realized he would always need someone to help him put on his pants.

Instead, the Librarian spent his days scowling in private and staring in public, feigning the occasional "I don't know where I am" eye-rolling, fooling many, apart from Manifesto the Great.

❖

It took ten years for the hippie colony to "spring up."

Ten years of raiding, several attempts at using water to create energy, two scarecrow wind collector templates, and the pulling of three spaceships, which, to be fair, was a blessing to the city and greatly appreciated by many, including Manifesto the Great.

In fact, the last spaceship was actually transported by the Foreigners, who, on the orders of Manifesto the Great, trailed it to a trading post on the promise of a new superpowered hemp full of hormones.

Finally, the days of ship-pulling had drawn to a close.

By the time Manifesto the Great was a teenager, James the Strong's strength had waned and he, struggling to pull spaceships, had taken to riding them, shouting, "Hurrah!"

Red with embarrassment, Manifesto the Great was on the verge of constructing a hijacking story when the Aliens jumped the gun and did him a favor.

The first few years were exciting for Aggie and the Aliens; they recycled, upcycled, and constructed like demons. Verandas were erected, greenhouses were set up, and plans for animal collection were in the making. A sort of Noah's ark of species to study and replicate until that is, the Liberty of Animal Front took hold.

Many in the city had little clue about the dwindling number of four-legged creatures; they just assumed they would always be there. That the influx of mechanical birds would eat the wasps, as intended, but not everything else that moved.

LM-2 pulled out all the stops to manipulate James the Strong: she talked of immunization against the wasps and the power of a needle. James the Strong took one look at the elongated affair of steel and glass, and fainted, going down like a pillar of books.

"Let's go with the mechanical birds," he muttered, coming to.

No one argued.

Aggie did her best to pursue her son.

When she assumed the time was right, she set up a secret meeting during a night raid.

❖

Manifesto the Great, trying to come to terms with a father who shouted "hurrah" way too much, was traumatized.

Walking into a room to find your dead mother not only alive but with a female partner and spouting the joys of veganism can do that to a young man, especially when caught in the process of "helping themselves" to whatever they wanted in the library *and* the Institute.

"We'd been blaming it all on the Librarian being scatty," said Manifesto the Great, "his brain being as useless as his legs, and all along it was you and your so-called women?"

Manifesto the Great rebelled, doing the opposite of whatever his mother suggested. He barbecued flesh like an enraged Viking, filled his rooms with skins of animals, and wrapped himself in fur and leather, breaking his mother's heart.

When his mother warned of the effect of too many mechanical birds, he ordered the making of more.

When she said the number of four-legged creatures was dwindling, he caged them. Soon, the mechanical birds had destroyed the natural rodent population, which had fed the larger creatures, and the whole animal cycle in the city had dwindled to the odd scurry of an oversized mechanical rat, circling mechanical birds, and a few penned animals—now infertile thanks to the soya feed.

Even the removal of the spaceships did not soften Manifesto the Great's heart toward his mother. In fact, he often blamed his mother for his father's slow descent into madness.

"We need more meat," shouted Manifesto the Great and ordered better feed—full of hormones to increase the number of offspring. He had no idea that mass-produced meat flattened the mind.

The Librarian, for the first time ever, tried to do something decent.

"We should stop eating these creatures and set them free," he said to the readers.

When the readers laughed at him, he turned to his leader. When James the Strong laughed at him, he turned to his prodigy. And when Manifesto the Great told him to "go lie down," the Librarian panicked, flooding the city with leaflets about the Liberty of Animal Front:

Please help us stand up to the leaders
and
save the animals.

The masses, inspired by the "stand up to our leaders" bit, went wild. They rampaged the city, the fields, and the farms, opening gates and pushing animals into freedom.

The only problem was, the animals had no idea how to be free; they trampled the grass aimlessly instead of eating it and had no idea how to search for water. The mechanical birds picked their dying carcasses off one by one.

The hippies, mid commune production, hijacked what creatures they could, but not much survived—mainly fish.

Chapter Thirty-Nine

A JUMP TOO SOON

"It takes more than a good catch to bounce an idea." -Librarian.

Ten years on

*W*hen the funeral celebrations were over and James the Strong's body was a mere smoldering pile of ashes floating by the waterfall, LM-2 and Aggie turned to each other with a look that required no words.

They had been watching from the room with a view, a place high above the smells of the bonfire. It was Manifesto the Great's idea; the last thing he needed was people realizing who Aggie was.

"My work here is done," muttered LM-2.

"Done?" said Manifesto the Great.

"Yes," said LM-2.

Manifesto the Great eyed her bags.

"You're leaving?"

She nodded.

Manifesto the Great looked down at the turtle parked in the royal transporter bay surrounded by curious readers.

"On a turtle?"

"Well, yes."

A reader poked the turtle; the turtle roared. Manifesto the Great tapped the window with a glare; the reader glared back.

The footman moved to close the blinds.

Manifesto the Great gestured a "leave it," then turned to LM-2.

"But what about me?"

"You?" said LM-2. "I slept with your father; I'm not sleeping with you."

Aggie coughed.

LM-2 blushed.

Manifesto the Great had come to terms with many things, but LM-2 leaving was not one of them. With a huff, he made to shut the window; it seized.

The footman silently closed it.

Manifesto the Great turned to Aggie. "This is all your doing, you and that Tarzan Tork. You've seduced my LM-2."

"I'm not your LM-2," snapped LM-2.

"How am I expected to rule when the people I trust are untrustable—keep leaving?"

"I had no choice," said Aggie.

"So you say," muttered Manifesto the Great. "So everyone keeps saying in this friggin' place . . ."

He stopped as the Librarian crashed through the door like a hospital trolley in A & E.

"There's a turtle out there!" he shouted.

Silence . . .

"Did you hear me?" said the Librarian.

"Did you know LM-2 was leaving?" said Manifesto the Great.

"Pfff, that," said the Librarian.

"What do you mean, 'pfff, that'? How am I to bounce ideas with no one to bounce with?"

"You can bounce with me," said the Librarian.

The adults eyed the Librarian like he was a child.

"Just because I am in a wheelchair doesn't mean I am unbounceable," he snapped.

"The last thing you can do is bounce," muttered a footman.

"Thank you," said Manifesto the Great.

"No one tells me anything anymore, let alone bounces things off me," said the Librarian.

He sped his chair into the room.

"That's because your memory is rubbish," said LM-2.

"I may have forgotten many things, but not the important stuff: *that* night, *that* accident, and *that* Cat."

The chair crashed into the desk; he reversed, and Aggie jumped out of the way, followed by the footman.

"That Cat had a kick like a mule," said the Librarian. He skidded past Manifesto the Great, skimming his heel. "And a yell that would wake the dead."

Manifesto the Great snapped.

"LM-2 is leaving, and all you can do is talk of the past?"

"The past is why she is leaving," said Librarian.

"He has a point, sir," muttered the footman.

No one said anything.

The turtle roared.

Manifesto the Great had had enough. "Leave us," he said to the footman, "and take that so-called Librarian with you."

The women watched as the footman made to push the Librarian, who resisted with a reverse onto-the-toes maneuver. The footman, with a curt lift of the wheelchair, saved his toe and reversed the chair out the door.

The door clicked shut, and after a series of "I can do it" slaps, the Librarian's wheelchair squeaked off into the distance.

Manifesto the Great turned to his mother and eyed her long hair. Over the years, he had heard her side, listened to her dreams, and forgiven her many things, apart from the hippie look she now adopted.

"Why did you come? Now the Librarian has seen you—he'll start rumors."

Aggie looked at her son. "It's time."

"Time for what, Mother, to cut your hair?"

Aggie's face fell.

She had planned this moment for many years—for him to join her, be part of their "new world"—but as she looked into her son's eyes, she knew it had been a futile dream. She had been deluding herself.

This was a man who believed that sperm pulled and ovaries obeyed. That sperm gave men the ability to lift things, move things, and yell a lot, while ovaries made women cry at the oddest of things and burn toast.

Tork was right. Her son was every inch her father's son.

She had seen him in action, poised on his special "height box" with a sermon that moved many.

He was a ruler like Arthur of the North.

She ran her hand along his cheek. *He has no idea that women are rising,* she thought. But there was still time; she could educate.

Manifesto the Great's face softened as he remembered those times as a boy when he could make her happy.

"Good speech," she said. "Your father would be proud."

"Pfff," laughed Manifesto the Great.

They both knew she was lying; the only thing James the Strong was proud of was his family member.

James the Strong's ashes were scattered at the foot of his statue. Men toasted, and women wailed until a holiday was announced—a holiday of dancing, chasing, and ravishing befitting the great ravisher himself, James the Strong.

Those in the city threw themselves into the celebrations and did their best to enjoy, which, thanks to the new super-deluxe hemp tea, most did, while the Foreigners, Aliens, and Aggie watched . . .

LM-2's innovative upgrading of a mirror having set spying on a whole new level.

EPILOGUE

There is more to a four-legged creature than a name: there's traits, phobias, and a fear of extinction."—Cat

LM-2 looked about Fanny's pristine office, a place where everything had not only its place but a label big enough to read six feet away.

Since the removal of the spaceships, they held their meetings in the basement of Fanny's man's office. He, thinking it was a knitting club, was happy to see the basement used—keep the mechanical rats out. He had no idea what Fanny was up to, which is what comes from listening to the radio rather than your woman at the breakfast table.

The door opened; Fanny appeared, arguing with a cleaner about the use of mops.

"They are not the same as bras," muttered Fanny. "There is no element of surprise with a mop."

"Surprise is not the be-all," muttered the cleaner. "In fact, surprise is a mere sneeze in the cold war of the sexes."

LM-2 laughed.

Her life had turned into something on par with a 1930s comedy, one of those delicious films Katherine Hepburn was in. In fact, she often dreamed of changing her name to Katherine, until Fanny told her names were superficial, using, God forbid, James the Strong as an example.

After the passing of James the Strong, LM-2 was not sure what to do and followed Aggie back to the Aliens' camp. Aggie had made it sound so adventurous, and Tork seemed so appealing. LM-2 thought they would all be like Tork. She pictured a big celebration meal full of women lean, mean, and, well . . . just like Tork.

She arrived at the eating area, stared at the row of grunting women, and realized that Aliens were as varied as the city folk and had no table manners.

She took one look at them eating with their hands, egging each other on for an arm wrestle, and decided one meal was enough.

"The city needs me," she said to Aggie, and Maisie jumped at the chance to escort her back and "cement" her connection with Fanny.

Aggie sat on the veranda, staring out into the sunset as the wind rattled the scarecrows. A black mechanical crow landed on its arm and blinked at her. She tossed a cube of fudge and laughed as other birds appeared, squabbling for a piece, until the turtle snapped at one.

The turtle minus her minibar was a completely different being. Without male and female hormones playing havoc with her pipes, the turtle had settled into a peaceful life of eating, transporting, and sniffing, until, after years of transporting and several clones later, she collapsed under the shade of a tree and didn't move except to snap at birds.

Watching her was the highlight of Aggie's morning. Well, that and Tork's wake-up beverage.

Aggie's heart was full; she felt almost blessed. Her son visited every week, often to bounce ideas off her.

His visits were always secret, aided by a lavish camouflage. It was the one talent the Librarian had never lost and the one thing that almost put a smile on his face: helping his prodigy camouflage "for the good of the city," despite the fact that he could not remember what "good for the city" was.

Manifesto the Great always arrived at sunset with a ceremonial flopping on a rocking chair and a sigh, waiting for the tossing of the fudge.

The first time he saw the turtle, he wondered why they kept such an old relic, until he saw the tossing of the fudge. He could forget his worries watching that turtle, and when he and his mother's "bouncing of ideas" turned into an argument, they simply shut up and tossed more fudge.

Tork appeared from inside with a "real men eat lentils" apron.

Aggie thought of all their conversations, arguments, and make-ups. Tork's "don't tell anyone" kindness, their dreams of a better world and better crops, and their fears for the city's future.

Tork was painting their kitchen, the first chore she had found where she could wear the apron without being seen.

It was a rubbish present from Aggie celebrating their abseiling anniversary—the day they flew across the city like Tarzan and Jane.

Tork had opened the present and, feigning a smile, handed Aggie hers: a hammer not even wrapped . . .

Neither were happy, and it took several hemp teas to "get in the mood."

The disappointment of presents was a yearly event for them both. Neither ever really got what the other treasured; Aggie had a box of tools that Tork used, and Tork had a series of aprons she didn't want anyone to see her in.

Tork stared at the sunset, absently wiping her hands across the "real men," hopeful that the wearing of the apron would lead to better things . . . to an early night after enough hemp tea to make rising early impossible and a repeat performance of last night's lovemaking a given.

She smiled—when Aggie was grateful, she was *really* grateful.

Tork kissed Aggie's head and slid her hand under Aggie's top, scooping her breast.

"See, not a drop of paint on your apron." She squeezed.

"I'm ever so grateful," Aggie sighed as her laughter echoed across the field.

****

Book 2 ***The Downfall of Manifesto The Great.***
is on sale now at your favourite store
Not sure? Then
Turn the page for a taste of things to come...

THE DOWNFALL OF MANIFESTO THE GREAT

Chapter One—The Orphan

"In the beginning, there was Beryl."—Verruca

1935

Beryl was discovered by an elderly reader sitting at the feet of the unfinished statue of her father.

Her mother, a woman with painted nails and love for lying in bed, had passed away moaning about her caffeine not being "hot enough."

Beryl had two choices.

To be swallowed up by the family groomed for a good match or do as her mother suggested and "run away."

She got as far as the courtyard of greatness and realized running away with nowhere to run was a stupid as the headless statue where she now sat.

"Sit at his feet," she'd tell Beryl, usually while Beryl was making her comfortable in bed, "it will lead to things."

Like what? thought Beryl.

She had watched the sun rise, and now it was going down; was she to sleep here?

Clutching her rucksack, she thought of a future with "the family," aunts preening her, telling her what a "no good" her mother was . . .

"Aunts are an earth's invention," her mother used to say, and "you are more him than me."

She wondered if she should go back, take her chances.

She hardly noticed the reader until he stopped.

He looked at the shivering child; her face was familiar, like a colleague he'd worked with years ago in the good old days, when things were easier . . .

She caught his eye.

"My mother told me to wait here," she said.

He looked at her solemn face; she was not even ten.

"At my father's feet," said Beryl.

"Squirt was your father?" said the reader.

Beryl nodded.

"And your mother was that woman?" He whistled through his teeth.

Beryl was one of the last to be born from a man; infertility had ripped through the city like a plague of smallpox, and no one knew why, despite the Librarian pointing to the food chain, but then who listened to the Librarian?

He could see she was special.

She had the intelligent look of her father and the intriguing face of her mother. A heady mixture for an elderly gent who liked intelligent females that were "easy on the eye."

Beryl's father was from the right side of the tracks, who used his head to make profits and mold Beryl's "gullible" mother before she went, well . . . mad.

The reader, a man with no partner and no desire for one, eyed this slip of a girl.

She had potential; he thought maybe even replace that "I have an answer for everything" LM-2, and god knows Manifesto the Great could sure use a new one of her.

Manifesto the Great's ideas were anything but brilliant; in fact, most pissed off the women, sparking "sit-ins" and "sit-outs"—codes for "no bed-diving," which Manifesto the Great in his wisdom blamed on the lack of children; perhaps this Beryl could change things?

If he had known what Beryl's true potential was, he would have sent her to the Art Centre, where children were welcomed, had the freedom to argue, and soon learned it didn't get them anywhere.

But he didn't; instead, he took her back to the Building of Opulence, placed her under the wing of the Librarian, a decision that in the end was the true downfall of Manifesto the Great.

In the ten years of Manifesto the Great's reign, the city had changed into "us and them"; "us" being the readers who ruled and "them" being the rest who bore the brunt of the readers' decisions.

Even though fewer babies were born every year, that less fish swam the rivers, that hills had turned barren, the readers, true "eat drink and be merry" followers, were deaf to any warnings, apart, that is, from the new chairman . . .

There was not even a shellfish to scavenge or a leg to barbecue; flesh-eating had become a luxury and noisy kindergartens a distant memory. All that was left was the odd scraggy four-legged creatures hidden deep in the hills.

Meat was rationed on par with World War II restrictions, sparking off fights over sausages, brawls at barbecues, and demonstrations on par with a four-legged stampede.

The city missed its barbecues and cheese, and, for once, the leaders could do little to help. It wasn't long before hunting and fishing became a distant memory, and meat went underground, illegally stashed under counters and traded in alleyways.

The Librarian, a man not partial to the "eat drink and be merry" philosophy, had warned, but who listened to an elderly man in a wheelchair, especially a man with a passion for wigs? Then when word got out of favors being traded for prawns and giblets, something had to be done.

Manifesto the Great, a positive man, instructed the institute to work on a robust form of fertilization.

The institute came up with growth food, which led to animals large enough to eat within weeks but with flesh toxic with hormones and bland as the Librarian's jokes.

The "new meat," still in its infant stage, was rationed to men under the belief that man's seed was the cure to the whole bugger-all *babies* issue.

Not exactly a popular ruling.

"What about the women?" said the Librarian.

"Let them eat mush," said a voice from the back.

"Here, here," chorused a few.

The Librarian looked at the idiots around the table. "You honestly think a woman is going to eat mush while grilling a chop for her man?"

"Great decisions," said the chairman with an eye on his leader, "are not always greeted with a round of applause."

****

On sale now at your favourite store

A NOTE FROM THE AUTHOR

I hope you enjoyed the rising of Manifesto Great. A stories inspired by my time living above an Indian restaurant and a huge need to use **Manifesto** in all it forms.
If you want to keep abreast of future Manifesto adventures then join me at...

www.kerrienoor.com
Or
Like me at...

 facebook.com/kerrienoorwriter
twitter.com/kezzamac
instagram.com/kerrienoor

The Rise Of Manifesto The Great

First edition. March 31, 2020.
Copyright © 2021 Kerrie A Noor.
Written by Kerrie A Noor.

❀ Created with Vellum